Cash Captured My Heart

Saved by a Boss

By. Tyanna and Jammie Jaye

Cash Captured My Heart: Saved by A Boss

Copyright © 2020 by Tyanna & Jammie Jaye

Published by Tyanna Presents

www.tyannapresents1@gmail.com

Synopsis

Loneliness is a hell of a drug. For Kyndall holding her husband Hakeem down came with the territory. Ever since high school but when disaster hits. The couple's relationship is tested, and the love that they have for each other is questioned. When conflict causes strain Kyndall wonders can they find their way back to each other, or will their love be lost forever.

Hakeem Richards always vowed to love his wife for better or worst. That was until things got hard, and he needed an outlet. When the lies and betrayal hit the fan, and his back is against the wall. Will Hakeem be able to get out of this web of deceit?

Cashmere 'Cash' Whitfield is determined to help his friends through this tough time, but when it puts a strain on his relationship, he tries to rearrange his priorities. When Kyndall starts to give up and Cashmere steps in. Cashmere's longtime girlfriend Nadia questions if there is more than friendship between him and Kyndall. Will trying to balance his love life, friendship, and business be too much for Cash to handle.

Take a ride with the crew in this story of lies, betrayal, and deceit. Nothing is what it seems, and no one is as loyal as they portray.

Chapter one

Kyndall

"Oooooooooooch!" I jumped out of my sleep, screaming.

"What's wrong, K? Are you good?"

"No, Hakeem, I'm in a lot of pain. I don't think I should be feeling contractions like this. I'm only six months."

"All right, well, come on, let's get to the hospital." Hakeem got up and put his clothes on, then he helped me get dressed, and we rushed out the door to get to the hospital. The pains were getting worse, but I was used to this. I already knew what it was, so I had prepared once again for the unthinkable.

By the way, my name is Kyndall Richards, and my husband's name is Hakeem Richards. We have been happily married for four years. Hakeem and I started out as high school sweethearts, and now here we are. After getting my breathing together, and not stressing myself out, we were now sitting in our car, ready to go. Hakeem got us to the hospital in ten minutes with the way he was driving. I could tell by the look on his face that he was worried. See, we'd been down this road before. I'd had two stillborns and two miscarriages, so the nurses and doctors in the maternity wing knew us.

"Stay right here, baby. I'm going to run in and get a wheelchair." Hakeem pulled directly in front of the hospital, then ran in. Five minutes later, he came running out with the wheelchair. He then let the security guard know he was going to take me in, then he would be back to park his car. The minute we made it to the door, I felt a big gush come out of me. At first, I thought my water had broken until I saw the blood running down my legs. All the doctors and nurses came running towards us. They hurried and got me on the gurney and rushed me up to labor and delivery. The pains were coming back to back, and I was in so much pain. Hakeem held my hand while they ran me to the labor and delivery wing.

"Mr. Richardson, how far along is your wife?" I heard the doctor ask.

"She just turned six months a couple of days ago."

"OK, sir, we are going to do everything we can to make sure they are both fine. Has your wife been pregnant before?"

"Yes, doc, and none of our babies have survived. They told us this time was looking good, and they gave her some type of shots. We were so excited because six months is the furthest we have gotten in a pregnancy." I heard the sadness in my husband's voice, and it broke my heart. I always felt like less of a wife for not being able to bless my husband with a baby.

Once we made it to the room, and they put me on the bed, the doctor came over to me and explained what he was going to do.

"Mrs. Richardson, you're doing good, and I'm glad that you are calm. Your husband told me that you're six months pregnant. Yes, this is early to have a baby, but at six months, babies are known to live. I'm going to need to check the heartbeat to see how we're going to proceed." The nurse hooked me up to the machine, and my baby's heartbeat was so faint, you could barely hear it. I knew right then and there my baby wasn't going to make it. The tears started to run down my face. Hakeem saw me crying, and he leaned down to kiss my forehead.

"All right, Mrs. Richardson, the heart rate doesn't sound too good, so we are going to rush you to get an emergency C-section." I nodded my head, and we were on our way.

An hour and a half later…

Hakeem and I were blessed with a baby girl. We decided to name her Nevaeh, which is heaven spelled backward. She was the only one of our babies who was born still living. Even though she had many complications, and they said she didn't have long to live, Hakeem and I wanted to enjoy these couple of days with her. Nevaeh's lungs were not developed, her heart rate was still weak, and she had bleeding on the brain. My little peanut weighed one pound and fourteen ounces and was fifteen inches long.

The doctor didn't see her living past today at the rate her heart was going. This was going to be the hardest thing that Hakeem and I had ever been through. True, we had two stillborns and two miscarriages, but to actually see and hold our little baby while she still had breath in her, and knowing that she was not going to be here with us long was going to crush both of us.

"Look at our little princess. She is so small, Kyndall," Hakeem said, bringing me out of my thoughts. They didn't want me out of bed because of the meds they had me on, but I needed to see my baby, so they put me in a wheelchair and rolled me down. Seeing my baby hooked up to all those tubes had me in tears.

"All those tubes hooked up to her little body." I cried as Hakeem rubbed my back.

"I know, baby, I know. Stop crying, and let's just enjoy our last days with her." This shit was easier said than done, but I knew my husband was right. While I stared at my baby girl, I prayed and prayed that God would hear me. I didn't know why this kept happening to me, but I knew it was taking a toll on me. This was the last straw for me. I didn't think I could go through this anymore. I was supposed to get on birth control the last time I was pregnant, but Hakeem didn't want me to. I was getting on something this time; I couldn't keep taking myself through this. Shit, you would think he would want me on something since he feels just as much pain as me.

Cash

"Mm-hm, just like that, Nadia. Suck this dick." I was leaned back in my bed, getting the best head ever. Once my dick touched the back of her throat, I knew I was about to shoot these seeds down her throat. Nadia's nasty ass looked up at me, smiled, and wiped her mouth. While I was in a zone, leaned back on the bed with my eyes closed, I felt my phone hit me in my chest.

"FUCK! What you do that for, Nadia?"

"Ya side bitch calling your phone." I looked down at my phone and saw that it was my best friend, Kyndall. Nadia hated her, and she swore up and down that we had something going on. I had to explain to her that me, Kyndall, and Hakeem had grown up together. We were friends, nothing more.

"Come on, ma. Why are you always starting that dumb shit? I just bust the best nut ever, and you can't even let me enjoy the moment."

"Fuck you, Cash!" Nadia barked while heading to the bathroom. Once she exited the room, I called Kyndall back.

"Yo, bighead, what's up?"

"Hey, Cash, did you get any of Hakeem's messages last night?"

"Nah, I'm just now picking up my phone for the first time since I walked in the crib last night."

"I knew you didn't get the messages. Well, I'm in the hospital. I had the baby last night. Things are not looking good for her, but she is still alive as of now. Cash, I'm trying to stay strong for my husband and me. I can tell Keem is going through it. He hasn't said anything to me; all he's been doing is staring at the baby and crying. I think he's shed more tears than me."

"Wow, K, I'm so sorry to hear that, sis. I'll be up there as soon as I get dressed."

After I assured Kyndall I would be up there soon, I jumped up and headed to my closet to find something to wear.

"Where are you going? I thought we were spending time together today."

"I need to get to the hospital with Keem and Kyndall. They had the baby last night and the baby not doing too good. Are you coming with me?" I knew she didn't want to come, but I knew asking was the right thing to do. See, I'd tried for years to get Nadia to be cool with Kyndall and Hakeem. Well, she seemed to be cool with Keem, she just wasn't trying to be cool with Kyndall.

"I'll go as long as you don't plan on staying all day."

"Look, Nadia, my friends need me right now. This is a hurtful situation for them. Hell, this shit hurts me as well, and if you're supposed to be my lady, you should be right by my side. I don't know how long you plan on not liking Kyndall, but we've been friends since high school. It's not like I'm just friends with her. It's not like I give you any type of reason to think we have something going on. That's my man's FUCKING wife. How many times do I have to argue with you about this shit?" I barked and headed to my bathroom to take care of my hygiene. After taking a piss, I turned the shower on to the temperature I liked before I jumped in.

My name is Cashmere 'Cash' Whitfield, and I'm a twenty-nine-year-old boss nigga. I was born and raised in Camden, New Jersey, where I sold drugs for years. I wasn't your typical street nigga. I slung dope, I sold crack, and I sold pills, all throughout middle school and high school. While the boys I ran with were standing on the corner all day, I was getting my education. See, I planned on getting out of this drug shit and still being able to make fast money. As of right now, I owned a couple of profitable independent pharmacies.

When I finished high school, I went to school to be a pharmacist. Yeah, I know what you all are thinking, and you all just may be right. I used my business and what I do for a living to still keep my pill flow going in the streets. I had everything set up so nothing would lead back to me or my business.

The draft from the shower curtain being pulled open brought me out of my thoughts.

"Cash, I'm sorry, baby. I didn't mean to get you upset. I'll go with you to the hospital." Nadia came in the bathroom and apologized.

"All right, baby, I'll be out in a second. You done opened the damn shower curtain, and now my ass is cold as hell." She winked at me, then smiled before she closed the shower curtain.

My girl was bad as hell, but the shit with Kyndall always turned me off. The shit was getting old as hell, and annoying. I was not going to keep going back and forth with her over this shit. I'd been doing it for two years. Yeah, we'd been together for two years now. Shit, Kyndall was the reason I gave this relationship thing a chance. I was the nigga who was fucking and ducking, and she put it in my head that I was getting too old for the shit, then I talked to Hakeem about it, and he felt the same. He told me that dipping into different pussy every other day gets old. When he told me that, I gave him the side-eye, but it actually wasn't bad at all, and it cut down on all the drama.

Shit, in my hoe days, I stayed in bullshit, but for the past two years, life had been good. I just hoped that Nadia didn't run me away with her bullshit. The water started to get cold as hell, which meant my ass had been in the damn shower too long. I turned the water off, dried my body, then wrapped the towel around my waist. When I made it to my room, Nadia had my clothes laid out on the bed for me, which was cool with me. I was shocked to see a pair of grey sweats, but then I remembered her little ass was going to be with me all day, so that was why she didn't care about me wearing them today. Once I was fully dressed, I brushed my hair, sprayed some cologne on, then headed out of my room. When I made it downstairs, Nadia was sitting in the living room, waiting for me.

"You ready, mama?"

"Yes, and I'm hungry. Can we stop to get something to eat?"

"Yeah, I'm hungry, too." She jumped up and walked over to me and kissed my lips. I swear if it weren't for her insecurities, we would be just fine.

Chapter two

Nadia

I really didn't want to go to the hospital with Cash, but I didn't trust Kyndall. I didn't care what he said, that bitch wanted him. I could see it in her eyes. I remember the first time I met her, she came over to his house unexpectedly. The bitch used his key and walked into the house in the middle of me sucking his dick. She gave me the nastiest look like I was a street hoe or something. He swore that she was looking like that because she was shocked, but I knew it was because she wanted to be the one sucking his dick.

"Baby, what do you want?" Cash asked, pulling me from my thoughts. We were in the line at Burger King. He knew I hated eating fast food. I wanted to go somewhere and sit down. Hell, the damn baby was here, and if it died before we got there, that meant we didn't have to be there long.

"I really wanted Perkins."

"Well, I can take you back to the house, and you can get in your own car and get what you want, or you can just order from here. You are wasting time. I need to get to the hospital, so again, what do you want?" he yelled. I wanted to say something crazy, but I knew that he was in his feelings, and I didn't have time to argue.

"French toast," I mumbled. After we got the food, we headed to the hospital. Just as we were pulling up, my text notification went off.

Dre: What's up?

Me: Nothing, with my dude. I'ma hit you up later.

Dre: All right.

When I looked up, Cash was looking straight at my phone. I prayed he hadn't seen the name. I couldn't have him thinking that I was up to no good. He was my meal ticket. My baby was paid. I had never met a man who had legal and illegal money. I knew the day that I met him that he was going to be my ticket away from the fucked up life that I had lived for the past twenty-two years. My life had been the worst, and my crackhead mother and father were the cause of it all. For as long as I could remember, they had used my body in exchange for dope. I was their ticket to get high. I remember the first time they made me have sex; I had to be like nine. I still have nightmares about that night. For the life of me, I couldn't figure out why they would do that to me, and that was one of the reasons I didn't ever want kids.

"Come on," was all he said before getting out the car. I knew then that he had seen the messages because he didn't come and help me out the car. That wasn't normal at all. He always held doors for me, and he never walked in front of me, always behind. I got out the car and headed to the hospital, and he was nowhere in sight. I pulled out my phone and called him, but he sent me to voicemail. I sighed and headed to the reception desk, so I could see what room his hoe was in. After the girl told me what room she was in, I headed to the elevator. As soon as I stepped off the elevator, I laid eyes on Keem's fine ass. I mean, Cash was the shit, but Keem was a real nigga. He was a nigga you knew had a little hood in him, but he was a well-educated businessman. To me, that shit was the ultimate turn on. I didn't know how Kyndall's stuck up ass had even pulled a nigga like him.

"Hey, Keem. How's the baby doing?" I asked as if I really gave a fuck.

"It's not looking too good."

I could tell that he had been crying, and that made me feel a little bad for him. I watched him as I walked off towards the waiting area. That nigga even walked with swag. If he wasn't Cash's best friend, I swear I would shoot my shot.

I headed to the room Kyndall was in. When I walked in, Cash was sitting on the edge of the bed, hugging her. You would have thought it was their baby who was dying.

"Umm-hmm." I cleared my throat so I could alert them that I was in the room, and so that he would know that he was doing too much. Neither of them paid me any attention, and that shit rubbed me the wrong way. How would she feel if she walked into a room and I was hugged up with her man? After today, I was ending this so-called friendship they had. He was going to have to choose: her or me.

As bad as I wanted to cut up, I knew it wasn't the time or place, so I just took a seat. I sat back and watched as he catered to her. That was Keem's job, and he was out in the hall, crying like a little bitch. Damn, it was just a fucking baby; get over it and have another one.

I got up and walked out the room because I couldn't take any more. He was never that attentive to me. It was more like suck it up and get over it when shit happened to me. I was so into my phone that I walked dead into someone. When I looked up, I locked eyes with the finest old man I had ever laid eyes on.

"Excuse you." I rolled my eyes.

"Damn, you too pretty to be so fucking rude. Get the fuck out my way," he roared and walked off. I watched him until he was no longer in my sight. Once I couldn't see him, I pulled out my phone so that I could call an Uber. There was no way I was going to sit around and watch them all day. Shit, I could be somewhere getting fucked. I had wanted to see what Dre's head game was about. I know y'all are wondering why I was cheating on Cash. Well, the answer is simple: I needed to have several backup plans. There was no way I was going back to my old life that I lived. I texted Dre and had him send me his address. He was going to be my next plan of action. I needed to add him to my roster, fast. I had a feeling that things with Cash and me were coming to an end soon.

Hakeem

"I told you I couldn't come today, damn Chrissy," I yelled into the phone. I was doing my best not to shoot off on her because it wasn't her fault that my wife couldn't carry a baby.

"But you said that we were spending the weekend together. I would hate for her to find out about us."

I knew that there was no way I could let Kyndall find out about Chrissy. She would kill me. Chrissy was my assistant, and I had been fucking her for the past two years. Kyndall told me when I first hired her that she would be a problem, but I didn't believe her. Times like this, I wish I hadn't started fucking with her, but every time she sucked my dick, she made me remember why I fucked with her.

"OK, give me a minute to figure some shit out, and I will call you," I assured her before I hung up. I knew that there was no way I would be able to pull this off. I knew that I couldn't use Cash because he was Team Kyndall all day. He would kill me if he knew that I was fucking off on Kyndall. He acted like she was his biological sister. The only option I had was to tell Kyndall that I had to leave on business.

Before we get into the story, I'm Hakeem Richardson. As you know, I am married to Kyndall. I work for one of the biggest accounting firms in the city, and I had worked my way to the top, and there was no way I was going back down. I also did all of the accounting for Cash.

I love my wife, but her not being able to carry my babies is a big issue for me. I know that I should just leave her, but that will never happen. She knows way too much, and I wouldn't dare let another nigga have her. I was a selfish nigga. She was mine, and mine only.

"Baby, how are you feeling?" I asked as I walked back into the room. She was sitting up on the bed, and Cash was sitting in the chair next to her.

"OK, I guess." The moment I looked into her eyes, I knew there was no way that I could leave and spend time with Chrissy. My daughter and wife were way more important.

I looked at her and felt bad because I knew that it wasn't in her control. The nigga in me still blamed her, though. I looked at the clock and saw that it was time for us to go visit Nevaeh. Earlier, they made us leave because it was feeding time. I prayed that when we got down there, they would tell us that she would be OK. I didn't think I could take losing another child.

"Y'all ready to go downstairs so we can see Nevaeh?"

They both nodded. Cash helped Kyndall up so that she could get in the wheelchair. When we made it down to the ICU, I looked through the window and wanted to cry all over again. I wish I could just give my life for hers. She didn't deserve what was going to happen to her. Deep inside, I knew that she wouldn't make it. She was so tiny, I was afraid that I was going to drop her.

I couldn't take looking at her any longer, so I took a seat in a nearby chair. Shortly after, Cash came and sat next to me. As soon as he wrapped his arms around me, the tears started rolling.

"I know this shit hard, but we are going to get through this together," he assured me. I knew he had my back, but I didn't think Kyndall, and I would ever get past this.

"I hope so, man. I can't lose my baby girl. This is the first time that she was able to give birth. I know God didn't bring us this far to take her away from us," I cried. This was one of the hardest things that I'd had to deal with. The other times didn't feel like this.

I looked up, and Kyndall was just staring through the window; it was like she was in a daze.

"Kyn, baby, you OK?" I asked, walking up to her. She didn't say a thing, she just stared off into space.

"Sis," Cash yelled out, and she turned towards us.

What? Why are you yelling, Cash?"

"So you didn't hear anything we were saying?" I asked.

"No, what did you say?"

"I asked if you were OK." I could tell that this was going to tear her down.

"I want to hold her," she blurted. Cash walked to the door so he could get the nurse's attention. He said something to her, and she went back in the room. Shortly after, the doctor came out. He explained what we needed to do before going in and holding our baby. We followed the process that he told us, and then we entered the room.

When Kyndall picked Nevaeh up, she smiled for the first time today. I sat back and watched as she talked to her. It was the most beautiful thing that I had ever seen.

"You ready to hold her, baby?" Kyndall asked. I nodded and took a seat next to her. She passed me Nevaeh, and then adjusted herself in the wheelchair she was sitting in. I looked at my baby and prayed that God made a way for her.

After staying in the room for almost thirty minutes, they told us we had to leave. We both kissed her one last time before going back to Kyndall's room. Once we were in the room, I cut my phone off because I knew Chrissy would be calling.

Kyndall needed me more than anything right now so Chrissy could do what she needed to. The only thing that was on my mind was keeping Kyndall from falling into a deep depression.

"I'm going to head to the house for a minute. Call me if y'all need me. I will be back later. Kyndall, text me and let me know what you want to eat and I will bring it back," Cash explained. We both just nodded. After he was gone, I climbed into the bed with Kyndall and held her until she fell asleep.

Chapter three

Kyndall

Today I got to hold my baby, and it meant the world to me. Things still weren't looking good for her, but I was still holding on. I had an awesome support system; Keem and Cash were the best. To be honest with y'all, they were the only real friends I had. I didn't do girlfriends because bitches were always grimy. I was close to my cousin, Shawnee, but she hadn't made it into town yet. She was away on business when I was rushed to the hospital, so that was why I hadn't called her. When I finally let her know what had happened, she cursed me out for not calling her.

"You good, baby?" Keem asked.

"I'm all right, Keem, just trying to wrap my mind around everything. I was thinking maybe we should start looking into adopting. I can't keep taking myself and my body through this. This is it for me, Keem. I just can't do this anymore," I cried. Hakeem rubbed my back while I let it all out. He didn't respond, so I knew what it was. See, we had this conversation after my first two miscarriages. Hakeem wants kids of his own; he doesn't want to adopt. I seriously believe that if he had known I had these problems, he wouldn't have married me.

"Shh, baby, don't cry. We will get through this, I promise. We don't have to talk about this right now."

"Are we doing a funeral service for Nevaeh, or are we going to cremate her like our other two babies?"

"Kyndall, can we please not talk about this shit right now. My baby is not FUCKING DEAD!" Keem barked while running out of the room. I knew this shit hurt, but the reality of it was we had to make these arrangements. My heart was so heavy right now, and the worst thing in the world is knowing that my baby is going to die. My phone started to ring, bringing me out of my thoughts.

"Hello, who is this?"

"Hey, mama, how you feeling?"

"Hey, Shawnee. When are you coming to see me?"

"I'm almost there. I'm exactly an hour away."

"How's Keem holding up?"

"I just asked him if we were doing a service and he went off on me."

"Kyndall, my god baby is still here with us. There's no reason you should be talking about any services right now. Granted, we all know the situation, we should still be happy and cherish the little bit of time with her. I'm hanging up now because you don' pissed me off. I'll be there soon."

After Shawnee hung the phone up, I laid on my side and cried myself to sleep.

"Kyn, baby, wake up." I stared up into my husband's face.

"How long was I sleep?"

"For about an hour. Shawnee called and said she was stopping at Popeyes to get you something to eat."

"What about you?"

"I'm good, baby. I don't wanna eat."

"Keem, you need to eat, baby. I know this is hard, but we need to stay strong."

"I know, baby, I'm good, and I'm sorry for snapping at you earlier. I'm just not ready to deal with that part of this yet. I want us to enjoy our princess while she is still living. I just came from seeing her again. They said everything is still the same." I guess everything still being the same isn't too bad. That means she's breathing at the same rate she's been breathing.

"Hey, y'all!" Shawnee yelled while walking into the room.

"Hey, Shawnee. What's up, cuz?" Keem said while getting up to hug her. After she hugged him, she ran over to my bed and pulled me in for a hug.

"Hey, mama, everything is going to be alright. Whatever you need me to do, don't hesitate to ask. I cleared my schedule for the next couple of weeks. If any of these rich bitches need anything made, they better go find another seamstress." Shawnee was one of the best seamstresses in our area. Shit, she had people flying her all over to make shit for them.

"You didn't have to do that, Shawnee."

"Kyndall, don't tell me what I didn't have to do. You know I'll be here for you and Keem as much as I can. That's the luxury of having my own business; I can take off as much as I want."

"Thanks so much, Shawnee, we really appreciate that," Keem assured her. The room got quiet, then there was a knock at the door.

"Hello, Mr. and Mrs. Richardson, I'm Dr. Reece. I'll be the one handling your release papers."

"Wait, what do you mean release? I'm not leaving here without my baby."

"Mrs. Richardson, you're not being released today. Since you had the C-section, you have to stay for a couple of days longer so your release day will be in three more days. Your pediatrician will explain to you everything that's going on with the baby. I just wanted to come introduce myself and let you know when you will be released. The pediatrician will also come to talk with you today about the baby's birth certificate."

"OK, doc, thank you so much for coming to talk to us," Keem said. I guess he could feel me getting upset, so he took over with talking to the doctor. Once the doctor was finished, he left, and I was ready to go see my baby again.

"Keem, can we please go see Nevaeh again?" He walked over to me and helped me get up to sit in the wheelchair. Then me, him, and Shawnee headed down to see our princess. I didn't know what the pediatrician had to say, but if I couldn't take my baby home, then I wasn't leaving. If her days were numbered, I was going to be right here by her side until she left to go to heaven.

Cash

Nadia thought a nigga was crazy. I saw her phone say Dre, but I was going to let her hang her-fucking-self. I was going to let her do her with Mr. Dre and get all caught up, then I was going to kill his ass right in front of her. All this time, she had been accusing me of cheating, and she was the one cheating. Dre's name came up a while ago, but I hadn't heard it anymore, which was why I didn't act on it. The bitch even left the hospital in an Uber, trying to act like she was mad at me catering to Kyndall. I swear I was fuming, and this was the main reason I didn't want to do this relationship shit. Since I didn't have shit to do, I decided to visit my mama. It took me fifteen minutes to get to her crib, and once I arrived, I parked my car right behind hers. The front door was already open, but the screen door was locked.

"Mama!" I yelled inside to get her attention. She ran to the door and opened it for me.

"Hey, baby, what brings you over here?"

"Hey, mama. I just wanted to see my favorite lady." When I walked in, she had a bunch of little kids laying on mats.

"Shh, don't wake my kids up."

"Mama, when you gon' let me get you a center? You're running out of space in here."

"All right, baby, you can do it as soon as you're ready." I was so happy she was finally letting me do something for her. My mother had been telling me no for years about letting me buy her a center for her daycare center. She'd been running this center out of her home for many years, and it was time for her to have her own building.

"What? You finally gon' let me take care of you?" She smiled at me and headed into her kitchen.

"Only because you're right. I do need a bigger space. Where's that damn girlfriend of yours?"

"She got mad while I was at the hospital with Keem and Kyndall, and she left. So, I don't know where her insecure ass is."

"What's wrong with Kyndall?"

"She had the baby last night."

"Oh, my. It was too soon for her to have the baby. How's the baby doing, and what did she have?"

"She had a little girl, and they already told them that she's not going to make it. She has too many complications, but as of now, she's hanging in there. Her name is Nevaeh."

"Aw, that is so sad. Tell her I send my love." My mama loves Kyndall and Keem, but she really took a liking to Kyndall. I guess because she never had any girls.

"I will try when I go back up there to see her before I head home."

"Son, I never get in your business, but that Nadia is no good for you. She doesn't even accept your friends. They've been around for damn near your whole life, way before her stuck up ass. If she means you no good, leave her alone, son."

"I know, mama. I'm already on to Nadia. Trust me, her time is almost up."

"Good, because I wish you find you a good wife and give me some grandkids." I chuckled because my mom said that every time I come to visit her.

"Mama, every time I come over here, you hit me with the wife and kids stuff. To be honest with you, I don't think I'm ready for all that just yet."

"Please, that's because you haven't met the right girl yet. When you find that one you can't sleep without, you'll be ready for some kids." All this time we'd been sitting here talking, I hadn't even thought to ask where my pops was.

"Where's Dad?"

"He had to go out of town with your uncle. They're trying to get another restaurant started in Memphis." My Uncle Paul lived in Memphis, so I guess he would run the restaurant down there.

"That's what's up. They doing big things I see. I'ma call him later for not telling me he was going out of town."

"He was in a rush last night, but I'm sure he will call you when he gets settled. Are you hungry? Do you want me to make you something to eat?"

"Yeah, you can. I'ma chill here with you for a minute anyway." Since I had no other plans, I was going to chill and talk to my mom a little while. Shawnee had taken Keem and Kyndall some food, so I didn't need to rush back up there.

Chapter four

Shawnee

When I got the call that she had given birth, I just knew what was about to happen. My cousin had been through this so many times. I knew she was going crazy, so I put everything on hold so I could be there for her. There was no way I was going to let her go through this alone.

"Kyndall, you need to eat."

"I'm not hungry," she whined. I knew she was going to say that shit. Every time this shit happened; she would go days without eating. That wasn't going to happen this time, though.

"How you gon' tell Keem that he has to eat and yo' ass not eating? That's backward as hell. Now sit up and eat before I call granny," I urged. She rolled her eyes and got up. I knew she didn't want me to call Mom-mom Ella. Our grandmom didn't play. Kyndall and I were her pride and joy. Hell, I was surprised she was not up here now.

"OK, damn." She grabbed the food I had bought her and dug in. She was talking about she wasn't hungry, but her ass was eating that damn food like she hadn't eaten in years.

"But you not hungry," Keem jokes. She smiled, and that shit made me want to jump for joy.

"Well, I thought I wasn't. Don't judge me."

"Baby, I'm going to run to the house so I can grab my laptop and shower, then I will be back. Do you want me to bring you anything back?" Keem asked Kyndall. There was a look on her face I couldn't read. She didn't reply, she just shook her head no. Shortly after, he left the room. Once I double checked that he was indeed gone, I looked over to Kyndall, and she was in a daze.

"I'm listening," I blurted. She looked at me like I was crazy, but I didn't care. She was going to tell me what that look was about. I think she had forgotten that I knew her better than I knew myself.

"What are you talking about Nee?" she asked as if she was really lost. If I didn't know better, I would have thought that she really didn't know what I was talking about.

"That look that was on your face when Keem said he was about to leave. I know that look way too well," I assured her.

"I think he's cheating on me. I can't blame him, though. I can't even give him a baby," she cried.

"That's still no reason for him to cheat. When you get married, y'all make a vow to God that you will be with that person for better or worse, through sickness and good health, for rich or poor. He took that vow just like you did, so he needs to live up to it. Kyn, you can't let him get away with cheating on you. That shit is not cool," I explained. Maybe he was really going home to grab some clothes since he had been here overnight.

"I just don't understand what's wrong with me. Why can't I just have a healthy baby? All I want is to give my husband a child. I just want to be happy. I know that this is going to tear my marriage apart. I know he blames me, I can see it in his eyes. On top of that, he said that he was going to get his laptop. His laptop is right there." She pointed at the backpack that was on the floor. "He never leaves home without it." She was crying so hard, it made me want to cry because when she hurts, I hurt.

"Everything happens in God's time. God gives His battles to His strongest soldiers. You will get through this." She just laid her head on my shoulder and cried until she fell asleep. Once she was asleep, I stepped in the hall so I could call Cash.

"What's up, sis?" he answered.

"You got a minute?

"Yea, is Kyndall OK?" he asked. I knew he was going to ask that. I didn't care what that man said; he is in love with Kyndall. He caters to her every need. I didn't care what she needed, he was going to make sure she had it. He had been that way since high school. I mean, that nigga did not play about Kyndall.

"Yea, well, in a way. So, look, about an hour ago, Keem said that he was finna go home to get his laptop, but it's already here, so Kyndall thinks he's going to cheat on her. Now, I'm going to say this, Kyndall is my sister, so there is no way I'm going to let him hurt her worse than she already is. I will kill his ass and not think twice about it," I finished. He didn't say anything, so I knew that meant he was thinking.

"You need to get yo' boy in check. She thinks what he is doing is cool because she can't give him a baby," I added.

"I'm on my way," was all he said before hanging up. I knew he was going to come and see about her. I wish she would have dated him instead of Keem. Don't get me wrong, Keem was cool, but the love he has was nothing compared to the love that Cash has for her.

I headed back to the room and took a seat next to the bed and watched Kyndall sleep. Kyndall was so beautiful. I just didn't see what would make her think that she had to accept the bullshit Hakeem was on.

Hakeem

"I told you I was at the hospital with my wife. Why the hell you keep calling?" I yelled as I walked into the house that I had purchased for Chrissy. She was starting to get on my nerves. Sometimes, she acted like she was a damn teenager. I knew she was young but damn. At twenty-one, she should be acting like a grown-ass woman, not a little girl. I had met her one night while I was at the club with one of my homeboys from school. She told me that she didn't have a job, so I hired her as my assistant. Kyndall didn't like it, but I still hired her.

"I don't care what you were doing. What I have to say is way more important," she yelled, pissing me off.

"There is nothing more important than my wife and child, now you need to learn to stay in your lane before I cut your ass off," I yelled while choking her. She was pushing it. I dropped her on the floor and pulled out my ringing phone. It was Cash calling, so I knew that meant he was at the hospital. I hit ignore and focused on Chrissy. She was still on the floor, holding her neck like she was hurt. She was so damn dramatic.

"Now, what is it?" Just as she was getting ready to speak, the phone rang again. This time, it was Shawnee. I hit ignore again. I knew they were probably just trying to see where I was. Before I could put my phone up, it rang again, but it was Kyndall.

"What's up, baby?" I answered.

"You need to get back, baby," she cried. I knew what had happened. I headed for the door. I needed to get to my baby fast.

"Well, when you get done, you need to come back. We need to talk," was all I heard her say as I walked out the door. I jumped in my car and headed back to the hospital. I was happy that I had gone home and changed because I would have had to explain why it was more than an hour later, and I still had the same thing on.

When I pulled up, I didn't worry about finding a parking space; I pulled up to the door and ran in. When I got to the room, everyone had tears in their eyes.

"Baby, what's wrong?" I said, running to Kyndall's side. No one said anything. They were all just looking at me. I knew that they were all probably mad because I wasn't answering for them.

"Is anyone going to tell me what the hell is going on?" I asked.

"Our baby died while you were out doing who knows what. That's what the fuck happened. How about you just leave, Keem. You knew she didn't have long. What was more important than us?" she questioned.

"Nothing, baby. I was at home, taking a shower. I was headed back when you called. I was just stepping out the shower," I lied. She gave me a look that I couldn't read and then turned her head. I walked to the other side of the room. I knew she was pissed and hurt.

"Let me holla at you, bruh,"Cash demanded. I didn't object, I just followed him out the room. He headed towards the family room.

"Damn nigga, where the fuck you been?" Cash asked me as soon as the door closed behind us.

"What you mean? I told y'all I was at the house."

"Nigga, please remember that we been around each other since high school. I know when your ass lying, just like Kyndall does. So, where were you?" he asked again.

"I was taking care of some business. I'm here now, and that's all that matters," I said before walking out the door. Who the fuck did he think he was questioning me? I'm a grown-ass man, and I didn't have to answer to anyone, not even my wife. Just as the door was about to close, he grabbed me.

"Whatever the fuck you doing, you need to get that shit in line. I see it, and I know Kyndall sees it," Cash stated. That shit kind of fucked me up because I knew what he was saying was right. I was fucking up, and I needed to get my shit together. There was no way I was going to lose my wife.

"I'm going to get it together," I assured him as we walked back to the room.

Chapter five

Kyndall

My little princess took her last breath today, and Lord knows I wanted to go right along with her. I knew it was coming, but I didn't expect it to happen this soon. *Why was God doing this to me?* Was something I had been asking myself for the past couple of hours. Not only was I going through this, I felt like my husband was up to no good. I'd been feeling like he was cheating on me for a couple of months now. I never told anyone, I just kept it in the back of my mind. Today when he told me he was going to get his laptop, I just sat there, looking at his dumb ass. If he had just said he was going to get dressed, I probably wouldn't have suspected anything. I hated that Shawnee could read my ass; I swear we were more like sisters than cousins.

"You good, mama?" Shawnee asked.

"I'm OK, just trying to get my mind right, that's all."

"Did you fill out the birth certificate?"

"Yeah, I did it last night, Keem just needs to sign it. Can you tell him for me, please?"

"Come on, Kyndall. I said I was sorry, ma. I'm sitting right here, why do you have to tell someone to tell me something?"

"Keem, save that shit for someone who wants to hear it. You were going to pick up your laptop, and that bitch is sitting right here. I've been peeping shit lately, and I'ma tell you this one time and one time only. Let me find out there's someone else, and I'ma kill the bitch, then take you for everything you fucking got, and I mean that shit," I barked. Shit, I didn't know where the hell all that had come from because my ass never talks to him like that. I guess all the anger that had built up inside of me was starting to come out. After I said what I said, he just sat there with tears in his eyes. I knew he was hurting, but I didn't give a fuck. He could deal with it his way, and I would deal with it my way.

"Y'all need to chill out. You are both in your feelings because of what went down, and it's understandable. Y'all are husband and wife and y'all need to deal with the loss of your child together. I got y'all back, and Shawnee does, too, but y'all also need to have each other's back. It's time to make arrangements for my goddaughter's funeral, so do it. Come on, Shawnee, let me take you to get something to eat while they talk." Cash and Shawnee left out, and Keem and I stared at each other for a minute before he got up and walked over to me. My husband pulled me into his arms, and we held each other tight and cried like babies. Out of all the times we'd been through this, this time felt different. I couldn't put my finger on why, but it just did.

"Baby, you're all I want, so don't ever think there's someone else. Yeah, I'm hurt by all of this, but don't ever think you're not all the woman I need because you can't give me a baby. We can adopt if you want; we can even get a surrogate."

"Right now, let's just grieve over Nevaeh, then we will talk about all of this at a later time."

"OK, that's cool. Now, are we doing a funeral or cremation again?"

"I want a funeral, that way we can go visit her grave."

"I'm with that, baby. Anything you want. What happened, though? She was fine before I left."

"They said they went in to feed her, and she wasn't breathing." Once I told Keem that, he began crying again. I'd seen him cry before, but this time, it just seemed like he was hurting ten times worse. I rubbed his back to soothe him a little. We were both tired, and this was putting a strain on our relationship. My husband and I sat and talked for hours, trying to figure out how we were going to handle everything.

Cash

This shit was crazy. I had to pull Keem's ass in the hall to talk to him. He told me he wasn't cheating on Kyndall, but there had to be a reason she was thinking like that. After I dug in his shit, Kyndall did the same. I was shocked at how she had read that nigga. I knew it was all the built up anger she was dealing with.

"So, what's up, Mr. Cash? How you been?"

"I'm good, beautiful. How about you?"

"Good, just working and living life."

"Ya sexy ass still ain't got a man?" Shawnee was fine as hell, and what you called a boss chick. Her attitude stayed on one, and that was why I hadn't tried to hit. I respected her being independent and bossy and all that good shit, but I personally couldn't handle all that woman. We would fuck around and be toxic to each other, so I never tried my luck.

"Now you know I like to stay single; that way I can fuck 'em and duck 'em. No feelings involved at all. Shit, that's been hard to come by these days, so I've been celibate for the past five months."

"I feel you. Relationships are hard as hell."

"They're only hard when you're with the wrong person, baby. Speaking of the wrong person, you still with that tac head bitch Nadia?"

"Yeah, for now. She's on some snake shit. She thinks I don't know, but I'm on to it," I chuckled.

"Can I ask you something, Cash?"

"Anything you want, ma."

"When you and Kyndall gon' stop playing?" Shawnee said while laughing.

"Man, Shawnee, what are you talking about? Kyndall and I are just friends. She's like my sister."

"Yeah, OK," she said while putting a french fry in her mouth. We had decided to go to Red Robin to get some food.

"Yo, I swear I've never looked at Kyndall in that way. You, my mom, and my girl all think the same thing. Y'all need to stop that shit. Kyndall and I are sister and brother. Nothing more, nothing less." This shit was getting out of control with everyone thinking me and Kyndall were into each other. Shit had me second guessing my-damn-self. The rest of our outing was quiet. My phone rang, bringing us out of our thoughts.

"Hey, baby, where you at? I miss you."

"Eating lunch, then I'm heading back to the hospital. Where you at?"

"Home waiting for you."

"Where you been at, Nadia?" She hesitated for a minute before she spoke.

"I was at my sister's. I needed a drink to get my mind right."

"OK, whatever, I'll be home later." After that, I hung up without saying another word.

"Trouble in paradise?" Shawnee said while laughing.

"Nah, nosey ass. You still in everybody's business, I see."

"Gon' somewhere with that bullshit, Cash. So, what do you think about this whole situation?"

"Man, I hope they get past this. Personally, I think they need to adopt or hire a surrogate. Kyndall is putting too much on herself trying to have a baby.I know she wants to give the man she loves a baby, but she needs to think about her health and sanity."

"I feel you on that one. Maybe this time, Keem will be willing to adopt."

"Yeah, I hope so because I hate seeing them going at each other's throat and shit."

"Yeah, the tension is thick as hell, but I hope he's not out here cheating on her, Cash. She doesn't deserve that shit because she can't give him a damn baby."

"I feel you, Shawnee, and I don't think he is. Kyndall is just feeling some type of way about what's going on. I'll make sure they are both good, I promise."

"Just let ya boy know, if I find out about him doing my cousin dirty, I'ma shoot his ass." I laughed hard as hell at Shawnee's crazy ass. I knew she was telling the truth with her crazy ass.

"Chill, killer. That's why ya crazy ass ain't got no man: you missing half ya damn brain."

"Nah, they just ain't used to a real bitch like me who ain't letting them run all over me. I need a nigga who's gon let me wear the fucking pants sometimes."

"Don't nobody want no mouthy-ass woman who doesn't know how to stay in her place."

"I am not mouthy, Cash."

"Shit if you ain't."

"Yo, Cash, what's up, my man?"

"Hey, Luke, what's up, bro? I was about to hit you up when I left here." Luke was my nigga, and the only other person I was cool with other than Keem.

"Oh OK, I wanted a burger, so I decided to come here. Hey, pretty lady, I'm Luke, and you are?"

"I'm Shawnee. It's nice to meet you, Luke." These two fools were sitting here staring at each other like they wanted to fuck right there in the middle of the resturant.

"Stop looking at my boy like you ready to eat him."

"Shut ya ass up, big head," Shawnee fussed. Luke stood there and laughed.

"Nah, she's cool. I like the way she looking at me. Can I get ya number, little mama?" He smiled and handed Shawnee his phone. The whole time she was putting her number in his phone, she was smiling her ass off. Once they got done talking, I assured Luke I would hit him up tonight.

"Shawnee, I'ma take you back to the hospital to get ya car. Tell Kyndall and Keem I'll be up tomorrow, and if they need anything to call me." It took me about ten minutes to get to the hospital. Shawnee and I said our goodbyes, and I headed home. I had some words for little miss Nadia.

Chapter six

Luke

Later that night

For the life of me, I couldn't keep Shawnee off my mind. I didn't think I had ever seen a woman so beautiful in my life. I hope she didn't think I was some creepy ass nigga because of the way that I was staring at her, but damn. She had the perfect body and all. I knew that there had to be something fucked up about her. Her appearance was way too perfect. I could tell she had a mouth on her for sure.

"Baby, what are you thinking about?" my baby mama, Meia, asked me.

"Nothing," I said with an attitude.

"What the fuck I do now?" she asked. I didn't care about her getting mad. Just a few minutes ago, she was acting crazy. She did everything but be a fucking mother to my daughter. Joi was my everything, but it seemed that she meant nothing to Meia. All Meia cared about was going out with her hoe-ass friends and getting drunk. The only reason I was still fucking with her was because I wanted Joi to grow up in a two-parent household.

"Where is my baby?" I asked, getting up, heading to Joi's room.

"She's with yo' mama. I dropped her off when I went to get my nails done," she said like it was OK. The only time Joi was home was when I was home. I didn't say a word, I just walked out the door. When I got in the car, I pulled my phone out and called Shawnee.

"Hello?" she answered, sounding like she was asleep. I looked at the time and saw that it was almost midnight. I wish I had looked at the time before I called.

"Hey, beautiful," I greeted her.

"Hey, Luke," she said with a little excitement. You wouldn't have known that she was just sleeping.

"What you doing, baby girl?'

"Nothing, I just got in. I have been at the hospital with my cousin all day," she explained. I knew that she was probably talking about Kyndall. Cash had told me that she had just had her baby and shit.

"How's the baby doing?"

"She passed earlier today." Her voice was so sad. I felt bad for Kyndall and Keem, even though I really didn't fuck with the nigga. There was something about him that didn't sit right with me. Deep inside, I knew he was a snake. I had been telling Cash that shit for years.

"I'm sorry to hear that." I gave her my condolences. I didn't know what I would do if something would've happened to Joi.

"So, what you doing up so late?" she asked. I didn't reply right away because I didn't know if I wanted to tell her about Meia.

"I'm headed to get my daughter," I admitted.

"Aw, OK, how old is she?" Shawnee asked. That made me smile. I was happy that she was interested in knowing about Joi. Most females just cared about what a nigga could do for them.

"She's five."

"What's her name, and why are you going to get her so late?" she questioned.

"Damn, yo' ass asks a lot of questions. But her name is Joi, and I'm going to get her because her sorry-ass mama dropped her off early this morning at my mom's house and didn't go back to get her," I stated. I just prayed that didn't run her off.

"Well, I won't know shit if I don't ask. Why didn't you just let her stay with your mom? It's way too late for her to be out. She should be asleep by now."

"More than likely she is, but I don't like putting her off on my mom. I know that's her grandbaby, but she is not her responsibility. My baby mama doesn't give a fuck about my baby, and the only reason she had her was so I could take care of her for the rest of her life. What she doesn't know is that shit is coming to an end soon," I fussed. I was so done with Meia and her bullshit.

"That's why you have to be careful who you have kids with," she stated honestly. We talked for the next forty-five minutes about random shit until I pulled up to my mom's house. I ended the call with her as I walked in the door. I thought that I was going to go and get in the bed, but I was fooled. Joi and my mom were in the kitchen baking cookies like it was noon.

"Daddy," Joi yelled as soon as she spotted me. At that moment, all the anger I had towards Meia was gone.

"How are my two favorite ladies doing?" I asked as I picked my baby up and kissed my mom on the forehead.

My mom was so short, so I assumed I got my height from my dad. I stood 6'4, and she was like 5'1.

"We doing good, baby. We slept all day, so now we making cookies for you and her uncle Cash," my mom explained. All she and Joi did was cook. I mean, it was so bad that I had to get her kitchen redone so they could have more room. That kitchen cost me a hundred thousand dollars, but I would do anything for the two of them.

Just as I was getting ready to reply, my phone rang. It was Shawnee calling back.

"Who got you smiling like that?" my mom joked.

"Hello?" I answered, trying my best to hold the smile that was fighting to get out.

"What you doing? I couldn't go back to sleep, so that's why I called back."

"Nothing, talking to my mom and my little princess," I said while tickling Joi.

"Daddy, I'm not a princess, I'm Joi," she corrected me.

"Guess you heard that," Shawnee laughed. I was about to reply, but Joi took my phone and hit the FaceTime button.

I was smiling hard as hell because I wanted to see her face. When she came on the screen, Joi took over, asking her a million questions, She even went in the other room. That really amazed me because Joi didn't talk to people she didn't know.

I didn't worry about going after her, I just took a seat on the island instead.

"Joi is staying with me from now on," my mom said. I had to do a double take. I was about to shoot off, but I decided I would listen to what she had to say. "I'm tired of her mother dropping her off, and you coming to get her late. I just want to show you how sorry her mother is. I want to see how long Joi will be here before she comes and gets her. Does she know you are here now?"

"No, I left without telling her where I was going. I'm getting so tired of her," I voiced.

"Daddy, Nee Nee said we hungry," Joi said, walking into the room. "Look, Nanny, she pretty."

Joi passed my mom the phone. Shawnee was smiling so hard. I knew she was embarrassed. "Yes, she is, sweetie. I'm sending Luke to get you. I'm going to cook something really quick, so make sure you are ready when he gets there," was all my mom said before passing me the phone. I waited until I was out the door before I started talking.

"I'm sorry. If you don't want to come, you don't have to," I assured her. She didn't say anything, she just hung up. I was turning around to go back in the house when a text came through with her address. I smiled and headed to the car. I knew if my mom and daughter liked her, then she was going to be good for me.

Nadia

Last night, Cash came in here acting like he ran shit over here. Talking boo coo shit like I gave a damn. This was the second time in a weeks' time that he had come at me. He always tells me he knows what I've been doing, but he really doesn't have a fucking clue. This nigga stayed saying I was cheating and shit, but that was only because of what his ass was doing with Kyndall. Once again, he swears I'm a dummy, and I don't know what he and his so-called best friend have going on. Well, the hoe lost the baby, so I hope he is done running to her side. The funeral was a couple of days ago, and it seemed like we were over there more than we were home, and I was sick of going over there. Plus, me and her cousin, Shawnee, stayed at each other's throat the whole time we were over there.

"What's up, ma? What you in here thinking about?" Cash asked.

"Just thinking about the talk we had last night. Cash, I really love you. Why are you always accusing me of cheating?"

"Nadia, I never accused you of cheating, it's just that you always doing some foul shit, then you stay accusing me of messing with Kyndall. Usually, when a person is always insecure, it's because of what they out here doing. Kyndall and I are just friends, nothing more, ma. I just need you to believe that, and I hope you aren't out here making me look bad because you believe me and my best friend are sleeping together. I'm telling you now, you and that nigga or bitch gon' be floating some-fucking-where." I laughed and looked at Cash like he was a joke.

"Baby, there is no one else, so I wish you would stop talking like that." I smiled at him while climbing into his lap. Cash was a little on the crazy side, which was why I fucked with Dre, who lived like forty-five minutes away. He knew I had a man, but he didn't know who he was. I wanted it that way because when niggas found out who my dude was, they tend to stray away. I guess because Cash's name rang bells in the streets and they didn't want any problems.

"I hear what you are saying, Nadia, but you stay doing the most, making me think otherwise. Always remember don't shit get past me, so don't get caught out here with ya skirt up." Cash was so cute when he was jealous, and shit like this made my pussy wet. I wanted to suck the skin off his dick, then fuck his soul right out of his body. He'd been in his feelings, and we'd been at each other's neck so much, it had been a minute since we'd shown each other any special attention. Knowing that I didn't have any panties on under my nightshirt, I started grinding on his lap.

"Baby, I promise I ain't doing nothing. Why would I cheat when I got this bomb-ass dick right here?" I whispered in his ear while kissing and nibbling on it while my ass was directly on his dick. I positioned myself so that I could start playing in my pussy. I took my finger and put it in Cash's mouth to make it wet, then I started rubbing my clit, getting myself in the mood.

"Fuck me, Cash," I demanded while I rubbed my clit in a fast motion as Cash slowly fucked me with his finger. See, I was a foreplay type of chick; I did all types of shit for the dick. The effects of me rubbing my clit and Cash fucking me with his fingers had a bitch about to squirt all over the place.

"Mmm-hmm, move those fingers faster, baby. I wanna see that pussy squirt. Make that shit rain for me, ma." As Cash talked, he moved his fingers in and out of me fast. The shit felt good as hell, and my stomach started balling up into knots.

"FUCK, CASH!" I screamed as I squirted all over him and myself." Cash lifted me and slapped me on my ass, then he got up off the bed and took his clothes off while I stared at him with a seductive look.

"Toot that ass up for me, ma," Cash barked. I did as I was told and got into position. I knew after this, I was going to be sore as hell. I loved pain and pleasure; my freaky ass did all types of shit. Cash was blowing my back out, fucking me from the back and fucking my asshole with his finger. The sensation had me ready to cum already. I swear this man knew how to cater to my body. I know you all are wondering why I cheat since he's the whole package, and I guess I do it because he does it. I know he says he doesn't fuck with Kyndall, but I just can't seem to believe he has no feelings for her. They might not be fucking at the moment, but he can't tell me they've never fucked. I was not buying that shit.

"Cash, baby, I'm about to cum." After I said those magic words, I felt my juices running out of me.

"Me too, mama. Where you want this nut at?"

"Let me taste it, baby." Once Cash pulled out, I turned around and took his dick in my mouth, and he shot all his seeds down my throat. After we were both finished, we fell on the bed and laid in each other's arms.

"I love you so much, Cash."

"Yeah, whatever, ma. You love my doggy style." I laughed at Cash's simple ass and watched him drift off to sleep. While he slept, I decided to get up and run some bath water so I could soak my sore pussy. I walked over to my dresser to grab my Epsom salt, and Cash's phone was going off. I picked it up and saw it was Keem texting.

Keem: Yo, bro, what's up? I wanted to know if you wanted to go out for drinks.

Me: Sure, what time you tryna go?

Keem: About 9. I wanna spend some time with Kyn first.

Me: OK, cool, just text me the place and I'll meet you.

Keem: OK, let's just meet at that little spot downtown.

It was time for me to meet up with Keem's sexy ass and tell him my theory about his wife and my man. Shit, Stevie Wonder could see something was going on, so I didn't know why I was the only one who could see this shit. I erased the whole text thread from Keem, so Cash wouldn't see it, then proceeded to take a bath. I had a date with a fine-ass nigga, and who knows, I might get him on my team.

Chapter seven

Shawnee

The night I got up and went to Luke's mom's house was one of the best nights I'd had in a minute. We'd been talking heavy lately, and I was loving it. I didn't know where this was going, but I knew I was happy about it.

"Hey, mama, what you doing lying here in the dark?"

"Shawnee, I want my baby," Kyndall cried. She had been depressed since the funeral.

"I know, baby, I know," I said while rubbing her back. *Where the hell is Keem's sorry ass?* I thought to myself. I had been here nearly the whole day, and I hadn't seen him at all.

"I woke up, and Keem was gone. Shawnee I don't think he loves me anymore. " This nigga was starting to get under my skin. The only thing that kept me from saying anything was our Mom-mom Ella. She said it was none of my business, and that the way Keem was handling things might be his way of grieving.

"All right, well, listen, mama, you can't be lying around, sulking. I think you and Keem may need to see a grief counselor. It may work for y'all."

"Shawnee, I don't want to see a counselor, I just want my baby back, and if you came here to talk about a bunch of dumb shit, you could leave. I'm sick of you, Cash, and Keem trying to tell me what the fuck I need to do." The way Kyndall had just read me had me super hot to the point I wanted to beat her ass. I knew she was hurting, so that was why I was going to let her make it this time. She knew me better than anyone, so she knew I didn't take lightly to disrespect.

"Listen, cousin, I love you, I really do, and you know I'll do anything for you, but I'm not gon' take disrespect. Granted, I don't know how you feel because I've never been in this type of situation, but I still try my best to help you get through. So, I don't deserve that smart-ass mouth of yours. I'm gon' leave and let you do you, but when I come back in a couple of days, you need to have your shit together, or I'm gon' beat ya ass myself. I'm not saying you have to be done grieving, but you need to at least get up and wash ya ass and do your fucking hair. Ella ain't raise us this way." After I said what I said, I walked right on out her front door. I was really in my feelings. I had always bent over backward for Kyndall.

Once I got to my car, I called Mom-mom Ella. If nobody could get Kyndall right, I knew she could. One thing she didn't do was tolerate disrespect, and she would make Kyndall get the hell up and do something with herself. After I called her, she said she was on her way. I sat in the car and laughed at the thought of my mom-mom putting Kyn in line before I pulled off. The minute I started my car, Luke was calling me.

"Hey, beautiful, what you doing?"

"Nothing, about to leave Kyndall's house."

"Already? You usually stay over there for a while."

"She pissed me off, so I'm out."

"Are you hungry? I was about to head over to the Cheesecake Factory."

"Yeah, I can eat. I'll meet you there."

"OK, cool, see you in a minute, sweetheart."

All these pet names were making me ready to come out of this celibacy thing, and buss it wide open for a real nigga. I was going to chill, though, but Luke had a bitch hot and ready. Shit, I hadn't come across a dude who had me feeling like this in a minute. I might do the thirty-day rule, but fuck ninety days. That shit wasn't going to happen. Hell, I damn near wanted to give it up the first night we kicked it. Laughing at my-damn-self, I headed to the restaurant to enjoy the rest of my night.

Thoughts of Kyndall came to mind, and I was starting to get worried about her. This was the worst I'd ever seen her, and I hoped my mom-mom could talk some sense into her. Tomorrow I was going to look up grief counselors for married couples who are going through shit like this. Kyndall and Keem had been together for years, and I would hate to see this ruin their marriage. Shit, I used to say I wanted a relationship like theirs, but I was not as submissive as Kyndall. Keem and I would be fighting over all types of shit. I needed a man to tame my mean ass. I needed a nigga to tell me to shut the fuck up and sit my ass down. The minute you strike me as being weak and let me do and say whatever I wanted, that shit would turn me off. That was one of the reasons I didn't have a man now. Yeah, I was tired of being lonely, but I wasn't going to settle for just anything. Plus, I was getting tired of thinking I had found Mr. Right and he turned out to be Mr. Not. The shit was getting annoying. Mom-mom told me to stop looking, and one would make his way to me, and that was what made me decide to become celibate.

Twenty minutes went by, and I was pulling up the Cheesecake Factory. Once I found a parking space, I parked and pulled out my makeup case so I could make sure I was good before going in. I said a quick prayer before I exited my car. *God, please help me be a good girl and hold out. I know that it may not be thirty days, but at least help me hold out for a week, God. Amen.* After my little prayer, I sprayed Versace yellow diamond perfume on, then headed in the restaurant.

Kyndall

Hearing loud banging on my front door woke me up out of my sleep. I didn't know who it was, and I didn't give a fuck. I didn't want any company, especially if they didn't have my baby with them. I'd been lying on this couch since my baby girl's funeral. Some days, I got up and washed my ass, and some days I didn't. I'd even missed my OB/GYN appointment. Those assholes couldn't tell me why I couldn't hold a baby, so I didn't want to talk.

"Kyndall Lorraine, if you don't open this damn door." Hearing my Mom-mom Ella made me jump up off the couch, and run to open the door. Once I opened the door, she was standing there with a mean look on her face. I knew not to say what I was really thinking. I wanted my baby, but I didn't want to die along with her.

"Get ya ass upstairs and get in the shower while I make you something to eat." I didn't say shit; I turned and ran upstairs and did as I was told. When Mom-mom spoke, my ass always jumped. I chuckled once I made it to the bathroom. The way she still had that effect on me was so funny. Whenever she was around, I straightened up real quick. Shawnee must have called her on my ass. Thinking back to how I had talked to her put me in my feelings. I needed to apologize to her. I'd been kind of pushing everybody away, even my husband. He'd been trying to hold and console me, and I'd been giving him my ass to kiss.

What I was going through was a hard pill to swallow, and I didn't know how to deal with it. After turning the water to the temperature I liked, I jumped in. Letting the water run down my body, the thoughts of my baby girl came to mind, and the tears ran down my face. I'd cried plenty of nights, asking God why me and Keem. We had so much love to give a baby, and God wouldn't bless us with one. After washing and rinsing a couple of times, I turned the water off, then got out and wrapped the towel around my waist.

Once I made it to my room, I oiled my body, then threw something comfortable on. I put a big t-shirt and some tights on, then walked over to my sock drawer to throw a pair of furry socks on. While digging, I came across my ultrasound picture, and the tears started rolling down my face once again, then anger came over me. Next thing I knew, I was throwing everything all over my room, and screaming at the top of my lungs. I was now pulling all the dresser drawers out, throwing clothes everywhere. I even threw all the shit off my dresser. I was in such a rage, I didn't even know my mom-mom had pulled me in for a hug.

"Mom-mom, why me? Why can't I be blessed with a baby? Why is God punishing me?"

"Calm down, baby. No one knows why God does what He does, but just know your time for happiness and to be someone's mother is coming. You can't let this get the best of you, baby girl. This is not the end of the world. It's going to be hard, but I will do as much as I can to help you get through all of this. Stop crying and come on downstairs so you can eat something. I even made you a cup of hot tea. I'm going to stay here with you a couple of nights. Shawnee told me how you talked to her and that was not right, Kyndall. She's always there for you, no matter what, and I hope you're going to apologize to her."

"I know, Mom-mom. I didn't mean to talk to her like that. I've been so mean to everyone the past couple of days, even my husband. I know it's wrong, but I'm having a hard time dealing with this, Mom-mom. All I want is my daughter, and since I can't have her, I guess I just don't want to be bothered."

"That's not fair, Kyndall. You're not the only one who's hurt behind this. Yeah, you were her mother, but shit, we were all her family. Not only are we hurt for her, but we are also hurting seeing you and Hakeem going through this. Did you ever stop and think about how everyone is affected by this?" Mom-mom Ella was right, but how everyone else felt never came to mind. Shit, they didn't lose a baby, I did. They were not the ones who couldn't carry a baby for their husbands, I was. So, no matter what she said to me, I wasn't going to feel any different. The truth of the matter was, they all gotta go home to their happy homes while I was sleeping in my broken home. My home would always be broken until I could bare kids. Until then, this was a broken home, and no one could do anything to change how I felt.

I had to act normal and agree with everything Mom-mom had to say so she could hurry up and take her old ass home. I didn't want her here, but I knew she wasn't going to leave me alone until I got out of this depression mode. Shawnee's ol' ugly ass gets on my nerves for sending her over here. Now she was going to be on my back the whole time she was here, telling me what I should or should not do. I was definitely going to act like everything was cool so she could take her old ass home and leave me the fuck alone.

Chapter eight

Hakeem

Losing our daughter had really taken a toll on Kyndall. I mean, yes, it hurt me, but she was at home, depressed and shit. I had been trying to talk to her and tell her that things would get better, but she didn't want to hear that. It was like everything me, Cash and Shawnee were telling her went in one ear and out the other one.

"Baby, what are you thinking about? I just had a full conversation with you," Chrissy questioned as she climbed into my lap. My dick instantly got hard.

"I'm sorry, baby. I was thinking about work," I lied. When we were around each other, I did my best not to bring up Kyndall's name. It was like she hated to hear me talk about her. I was fine with that because, in a way, I didn't want to think about Kyndall anyway. The truth was, I couldn't stop thinking about my wife, I just didn't know if we were going to be able to get past this.

"Um, well, can I put something else on your mind?" she asked seductively. She Dropped to her knees and pulled my dick through the front of my boxers. I was getting dressed so I could go home, but as you could see, that wasn't going to happen.

As soon as her warm mouth wrapped around my dick, I was ready to nut. That was one of the things that made me want her so bad. Normally, when a nigga nuts the first time, it takes forever to get that second nut, and a third one is out the question, but not with Chrissy. Some days I nutted four or five times, and that shit drove me crazy. That was part of the reason why I couldn't leave her ass alone.

"Fuck, slow down," I damn near begged. I knew she wasn't going to lighten up because she wanted me to nut fast. I wasn't going to let that happen today, though. I grabbed her head and fucked the shit out of her face. I had wanted to do this for a while. When I noticed that she was trying to stop me, I went in. She was making all kinds of sounds, and that shit was turning me on. Before I knew it, I was releasing down her throat. Kyndall would never let me do that to her. Damn, there I go again, thinking about my wife. It was like I couldn't get her off my mind for shit.

Chrissy got up so she could get a towel to clean me. I took that time to text Cash and see what was up. I should have been going home to check on my wife, but that was the last thing on my mind. I just couldn't sit around her while she was depressed. That shit weighed heavily on my heart and I just couldn't do it. After he agreed to meet up with me, I cleaned myself off and got dressed.

"Baby, are you coming back today?" Crissy asked as she climbed in the bed, ass naked. I almost rocked up again, but I knew if I did, then I wasn't going to meet Cash. Hell, I wouldn't even be able to go home.

"Yea, I should. Why, what's up?" I asked. I could tell something was on her mind. She had been acting a little off since I had gotten here earlier.

"Um, there was something I wanted to talk to you about."

"Talk to me, baby."

"Well, I know that shit is hard with what you are going through with your wife, but I think I'm pregnant. I don't know for sure, but it's very possible. My cycle is two weeks late," she stated. I felt like someone had knocked the wind out my chest. I knew there was a possibility it could happen, but damn, I didn't expect it.

"What?" I asked. I didn't really want her to repeat herself, but I wanted to make sure that I had heard her right. This shit couldn't be happening to me. I looked into her eyes and saw an innocence I hadn't ever seen before. I knew then that what she was saying was all true.

"I THINK I'M PREGNANT," she yelled. I didn't worry about replying, I just walked out the door. This was too much for me. I seriously needed a drink. There was no way she was going to have my baby. I couldn't lie and say I didn't love her, but it was nothing compared to the love I had for Kyndall. There was no way I could hurt Kyndall like that. I knew that her depression would be at an all-time high if she found out I was not only cheating but had gotten someone else pregnant.

Honestly, I didn't think I would be able to live with myself if she killed my baby. I had wanted a baby for so long, and now I might have the chance to have one. I never thought I would have a baby with anyone other than my wife, but I guess I had to push that to the back of my mind. In a way, I was excited, I just prayed she would be able to hold a baby, unlike Kyndall.

When I pulled up to me and Cash's regular meeting spot, I didn't see his car, so I headed in and waited. After ten minutes, I picked up my phone to call and see where he was, but someone stopped me. I looked up, and it was Nadia, looking good as fuck. She was wearing a dress that looked like it was painted on her. As she made her way to the chair next to me, my eyes went straight to her fat ass. *Damn, I see why that nigga is crazy about her ass,* I thought as I watched her adjust in the chair.

"What you doing here?" I asked.

"That wasn't Cash you were texting, it was me," she admitted. I didn't have time for this shit. He knew damn well he shouldn't have let her near his phone. Hell, Kyndall couldn't even look at my shit.

"So, he doesn't know you are here? What's your reason for wanting to meet me?" I shot off question after question. I really wasn't giving her time to talk, but I didn't care. She was on some slick shit. One thing I wasn't about to do was be seen with my homeboy's girl. Cash was in the streets back in the day, so he knew a lot of people. I didn't need anyone calling him, telling him they saw me with his girl.

"We need to talk about your wife and my nigga." When she said that, she had my full attention. What could she have to say about my wife?

"Let's go somewhere else," I recommended. As soon as we walked out the door, my phone rang. I looked down and saw that it was Chrissy, so I hit ignore. I would just get with her later. I jumped in my car and Nadia did the same. I pulled up at the Hilton down the road, jumped out and got a room, then headed back out to get her. After I gave her a key, I told her to wait ten minutes and come up.

I headed straight to the bathroom when I walked in the room. I had been holding my piss since I had left Chrissy's house. By the time I came out, Nadia was sitting on the bed, looking through her phone.

"So, what's up, ma?"

"So, you really don't see it?" she asked. I knew then she was on some bullshit.

"See what?" I asked, pulling a chair in front of her.

"That Kyndall and Cash are fucking." She threw me off with that statement because there was no way that was happening.

"You tripping, ma. That shit ain't happening. For one, Cash is my boy, and secondly, my girl wouldn't cheat," I explained to her.

"If you say so. That nigga runs to her every beck and call. When she needs something, she calls him. He's around her even if you not. What do you call all of that? I have a brother, and he don't do as much as Cash does for her. How could you not see that?"

I had never looked at things that way. Everything she said was true, but I didn't think they would do me like that. We'd been friends for far too long for them to pull something like that.

"Naw, ma, you tripping. There is no way that's happening." I got up to leave, and she grabbed my hand. I looked at her, and she had the fuck me look in her eyes, and that caused me to rock up.

"Look, Nadia, you're my boy's girl, so you know I can't fuck with you like that," I assured her.

"They fucking, so why can't we," she stated more so than asked. I stood there for a second, which gave her time to undress. When I saw her body, I knew there was no way I would be able to leave.

She pulled me closer to her and then unbuckled my belt. My pants dropped to the floor, and that was all she wrote. We laid up in the room and fucked all night. When I woke up, it was five in the morning, and I knew Kyndall was going to go apeshit on me. I looked to my side, and she was gone. I guess she knew that Cash would kill her if she didn't come home.

I grabbed my shit so I could head home. I just hoped she was asleep upstairs and not on the couch like she had been for the past few weeks. On the ride home, I made sure to call Chrissy so she wouldn't be calling all day. I also needed her to know that I wasn't mad at her. We ended the call as I was pulling into the driveway. I noticed that Cash's car was there, and so was Ms. Ella's. *What the hell were they doing here this time of morning?*

I walked in the door, and Kyndall was on one end of the couch, and Cash was on the other. I didn't see Ms. Ella, so I headed straight for the shower. I knew they couldn't have been doing anything with her here.

Cash

I was sleeping good as hell until I heard the door open. I peeked and saw that it was Keem. That nigga came in the house and went straight upstairs. I looked over at Kyndall, and her eyes were filled with tears. I was hoping that she would have still been sleeping. I didn't want her to have any more to stress about than she already did. When she noticed that I was looking at her, she turned her head. I jumped up and headed upstairs so I could have a talk with Keem.

"Damn nigga, where yo' ass been?" I asked as I took a seat in the chair that was near their window.

"I just needed some time alone," he lied.

"Or did you need some time with Chrissy?" I asked. I could tell by the look on his face that he didn't think I knew about her. I'm Cash, I know everything.

"What you mean, Chrissy?" he asked. I just laughed. He couldn't think I was that damn dumb.

"Nigga, you know yo' assistant you been fucking for the past two years. You couldn't have thought I didn't know about y'all. Nigga, we have been around each other for a long time, I know you," I told him. He was still just standing there like he couldn't find the words to say.

"I know what you think, but that's not what has been going on," he lied again. I knew he didn't want me to find out because I didn't play about Kyndall. She was all a man needed. She had beauty and brains. What more could a man want?

There were niggas out here like me, wishing they had a woman like Kyndall. He had her and was dogging her out, and that shit was not cool at all.

"Damn, you talking like she ya girl or something," he stated. I didn't worry about replying. I knew he was going to hang himself, so I just headed back downstairs so I could go home and hear Nadia's nagging-ass mouth. She had been calling me since midnight, but I didn't answer because I was tending to Kyndall.

On the ride home, Luke called and said that he needed to holla at me, so I headed to his mom's house. I knew Nadia was going to trip, but I didn't give a damn. I was ready to dismiss her ass anyway. I pulled up to his house, and his crazy ass was on the porch, smoking. That meant baby girl was there, so I knew then it was about his hoe-ass baby mama.

"What's good?" He dapped me up and passed me the blunt. I took a pull before taking a seat.

"Shit, man, just trying not to kill my baby mama. I'm one step from kicking that hoe out my shit. My baby has been over here for a few days, and all that bitch worried about is who I was laid up with. Then, to top that, a nigga feeling Shawnee, but I can't push anything with her because of Meia. I just don't want to bring her in a toxic situation," he explained. I could see the stress on his face. I wanted to laugh but knew he would get mad.

Luke was like my brother. We met when I was in college. I used to buy weed from one of the niggas who used to work for him. The little nigga sold me some bullshit weed, so I went to get my money back, and that was when I met Luke. He thought I was just some college kid. He had no idea I was a straight savage until he told me I couldn't get my money back. I shot the little nigga who sold it to me, and that was when we found out the little nigga had gotten robbed and had gone and bought some weed from someone else so he could pay Luke back. We had been tight since that day.

"So you in love with the homie?" I joked.

"Nigga, don't be saying no shit like that. That shit sounds gay as hell."

"It's cool. Shawnee dope as hell. Her mouth is smart, but she got her life in order," I assured him.

"Why you ain't never tried to fuck off?" he asked me. I knew that question was coming. So many people had asked me that over the years.

"Honestly, Kyndall and Shawnee are like sisters to me," I simply replied. He was giving me the side-eye, so I knew what he was thinking.

"Nigga, I done told ya ass that Kyndall is not your sister. You know damn well you in love with her. That's why ya ass be ready to get on Hakeem's bitch ass." He did not fuck with Keem because he thought Keem was a snake.

"I'm not gon' keep telling you and Shawnee to stop saying that shit." I was getting irritated with that shit. Everyone wanted to tell me how I felt.

"Whatever, nigga," was my reply. I knew that if I said something back, we would be going at it all day.

"But I called you over here because I want to talk to you about this," he said, handing me a folder. It was the numbers for the month. I looked through the folder, and nothing stood out to me.

"What's wrong with it?" I asked. He got up, and I followed him into the house. We went to his office, and he cut on the monitor.

"So, as you know, I have cameras in all of the spots. This is the one from the warehouse. If you look at the date, you would see that this is Dre doing the count for the day. Look at the money machine, now look at what Keem has on the sheet," he instructed. I did as he said, and the number was almost five thousand off. For the next hour, we looked through the numbers. There was nearly nine thousand dollars missing, and that shit really pissed me off. I knew that it had to have been Dre because Hakeem wouldn't steal from me. He had been doing my books for years. He was the one who had helped me get this shit in line so I could clean my money.

My mind was all over the place. I knew there was no one other than Kyndall I could talk to about this. Shawnee didn't really like Keem, so I knew she would say he was stealing.

"Find me an accountant. We will have him go over the books and see what's going on before we react," I explained. I wanted to have all my facts in line when I went to Hakeem and talked with him.

We talked for a while longer, then I headed to the house. I was just praying that Nadia was gone because I wasn't in the mood for her bullshit.

Chapter nine

Luke

Cash swore it wasn't Keem robbing him. There was a possibility it could be Dre, but I still didn't put shit past Keem. If he was innocent, I'd apologize, but until then, I would be on his ass. Doing what Cash asked, I called one of my accountant buddies and got him on the job. I assured Cash that I would get back to him in about a week.

Once he left, I decided to hit Shawnee up, and have her meet me at my mama's crib. I was sick of meeting her here at my mama's. I wanted to take her to my place, but I didn't want to take the chance of Meia coming there. Then I didn't want to take her to my apartment I kept in the hood because Shawnee deserved better than that. I was glad she understood my reasoning for all of this. She and I had been kicking it heavy, and my baby even asked to FaceTime her every day.

"Daddddyyyy!" Joi screamed, running out of the house.

"Hey, little mama, what you want?"

"Nothing, just wanted to see what you were doing. Is Nee-Nee coming today?"

"Yes, baby, she's on her way. So, you like Ms. Nee-Nee, huh?"

"Yup, her so nice and pretty. Her let me play on her phone, and she said my daddy is handsome." While Joi and I were engaging in a whole conversation about Shawnee, we hadn't even heard her pull up.

"Shh, she's here. We can't talk about her anymore," Joi whispered in my ear. I swear my daughter was so smart. I couldn't do shit but laugh at her little-grown ass. When Shawnee walked up the steps, I met her at the top and pulled her in for a hug.

"What's good with you, beautiful?" I whispered in her ear while kissing her neck.

"I'm great, now that I see you."

"Hey, Nee-Nee. Come on, let's go see Nana," Joi said while grabbing her hand. All I could do was shake my head and laugh and follow them into the house.

"Hey there, Ms. Shawnee. I see my son can't get enough of you," my mama had the nerve to say. These two were so embarrassing.

"Mama, can you please take Joi to watch TV."

"Come on, little lady. Let's go watch *Princess and the Frog*." Shawnee and I were finally alone.

"Finally got you all to myself."

"That probably won't last," Shawnee said. I grabbed her hand and pulled her in between my legs. She then wrapped her arms around my neck and looked down at me.

"I'ma ask you something, and I want you to be honest with me."

"Go ahead. Tell me what's on your mind."

"What we doing, shorty? I mean, I'm enjoying time with you, and I really want to see where we can go with this."

"I feel the same way, Luke. It's just that I don't know if I can deal with baby mama drama. I know we haven't come in contact yet, but it's probably coming soon." Meia was always fucking shit up for me, and I didn't even want her ass. I hadn't even slept with her in about six months, so I knew she was doing her. Shit, I always had Joi, so there was no need to let her mooch off of me. When she had my daughter, I made sure the bills were paid, and she had food. Now it seemed like Joi was at my mom's house ninety-nine percent of the time.

"Listen, baby, I'ma be real with you. Meia stays on good bullshit all the time, and that's why we not together now. I want you bad as hell, ma, and I don't think I'll let you walk away because my baby mama acts childish. Just give me some time to work all this shit out, then I'm all yours without the baby mama drama."

"OK, handsome, I'ma hold you to that. Now, how about we leave here and go to my place?" What Shawnee was saying was music to my ears. I couldn't wait to get her alone.

"All right, cool. Let me go tell my mama and kiss Joi goodnight, then I'll be ready to go." As soon as I got up, there was a knock at the door. The minute I opened the door, I regretted every minute of it.

"Meia, what you want?"

"Luke, stop playing and let me in. I came to see my daughter."

"She's been here for damn near a week and you just now want to see her?" I let her stupid ass in, praying she didn't start any shit at my mama's house. Meia walked her big head ass into the house and sat on the couch.

"Mama, I'm about to head out in a minute. Call me if you need me for anything." While I was kissing my mom and Joi on their foreheads, Shawnee came in to say her goodbyes.

"See you later, mama, and cupcake, I'll see you later, too."

"Uh-uh! Luke, who is this, and what is she doing here?"

"Hold up, wait a minute now, Meia. Last time I checked, this was my house." My mama shut that shit right down before Meia even got started. Shawnee and I walked right out the door like nothing had happened.

"I'ma get in the car with you. I'll just pick my car up tomorrow." I didn't even give her a chance to say I was spending the night; she already knew what it was. We both jumped in her car and headed to her spot.

Nadia

I was lying in my bed, thinking about how Keem had fucked me right last night. When I got home about six in the morning and didn't see Cash, I wasn't in my feelings about fucking his friend at all. Shit, he was probably laid up with Kyndall any-damn-way. When I got in the door, I was sure to send Keem a text, letting him know that Cash wasn't home. He was going to believe my ass sooner or later. If it meant I was going to have to keep putting this good pussy on him, that was what it was going to be. Cash walked in while I was in my thoughts, but he didn't say shit. He stripped out of his clothes and headed straight to the bathroom. No matter how much this kitty purred, I couldn't have sex with him today. I had been with Dre and Keem back to back. I needed to soak in a hot vinegar bath and use my vaginal tightening gel. Cash wasn't getting any of this kitty until I was straight. While he was in the shower, I decided to let Keem know how good of a night I had. Also, I hit Dre up and told him I would see him in a couple of days.

"Who the fuck you boo loving with?" Cash came out of the bathroom with a towel around his waist.

"Nobody. I was looking at something on Facebook."

"Yeah, whatever." I was getting sick of his smart-ass mouth and attitude.

"Listen, Cashmere, I didn't do shit to you, so don't come in here with an attitude like ya black ass didn't just stay out all fucking night. Where were you? Let me guess, Kyndall needed you," I barked while leaving out of the room. Since I didn't have shit else to do, I decided to go in the kitchen and see what we had so I could make a big dinner tonight. I'd been out, acting a damn fool lately, so I figured today I would stay in. Thoughts of Cash came to mind, and all I could think about was where we had gone wrong. Shit was going so well the first year of our relationship, and now he acted like he hates me, and he's the one cheating.

Deciding on baked salmon topped with garlic butter asparagus, steamed shrimp, and white rice, I got everything I needed out and started cooking. An hour had passed, and dinner was ready, so I grabbed a bottle of Barefoot Moscato, then fixed me a plate and sat to enjoy my dinner alone. All of a sudden, I got in my feelings because I had a whole man upstairs, and here I was, sitting here, eating alone.

"So, you just gon' eat without me?" Cash said, bringing me out of my thoughts.

"I didn't think you wanted to eat with me since I haven't been one of your favorite people lately." Cash walked over to me and wrapped his arms around my waist.

"It ain't even like that, baby, and I'm sorry we've been at each other's throats lately. I don't know what it's going to take for you to believe that Kyndall and me don't have anything going on. I've been trying my best to be the man you want and need, but the nagging and accusing me of cheating is getting old, ma. There's no way in hell we gon' be able to have a relationship if we don't trust one another." Everything Cash was saying was true, and his sincere words were tugging at my heart.

"I'm sorry, too, Cash. I guess I'm not used to my man having a relationship with another female. It's like no matter what we have planned, you stop it all to go run to her side, and the shit is bothering me. Now, I'm not asking you to give up your friend, but what I will ask you to do is put a minimum on how much you run to her. The shit doesn't look good at all, and it's not fair to me. Shit, she has a husband, so why does she always need my man?"

"Well, how about I'll work on my part, and you work on yours. Are you willing to work with me on our relationship?"

"Cash, I'll do any and everything for you, baby. Now, sit down so I can fix my man a plate." I smiled and winked at him while I got up to fix him a plate. While I was making Cash's plate, thoughts of what Keem and I had done came to mind, and I felt like shit. From here on out, I was going to make a promise that I would never cross paths with Keem again. Once I finished making his plate, I poured him something to drink, then sat it all in front of him.

"Thank you, baby. Now, what are we doing after we eat?"

"How about we lay up and have a movie night?"

"I'm with that, and I'll turn my phone off. Tonight, and from now on, I'ma make sure I give you all my time." Cash sounded like he was serious, but seeing was believing in this relationship. We both sat, ate, talked, and enjoyed each other's time while we finished our dinner. It had definitely been a long time since we had done this, and I prayed we had many other times like this.

Chapter ten

Shawnee

When Luke told me that he was ready to see where our friendship went, it was music to my ears. Yeah, it was soon, but hell, I wanted this nigga. I had told him I wasn't dealing with this baby mama drama, and what do y'all know, his baby mama shows up right after our talk. She was pretty, but baby girl didn't have shit on me. She was trying to be messy, but Luke's mama set her ass straight.

"What you over there thinking about, beautiful?"

"How ya mama set Meia straight before she got these hands." He chuckled, then shook his head.

"Shawnee, please, baby, don't pay her no mind. Now, if she gets in ya face or puts her hands on you, I know you have no choice but to react, but if all she does is talk shit, please, baby, just ignore her. A queen never lets a peasant take her off her throne; always remember that." Hearing him say that made me smile, but I wasn't the type who ignored shit, so Miss Meia better stay in her place and not come for me.

"I hear you, boo, now what movie do you wanna watch?" I asked. We had eaten dinner and were now cuddled up on the couch under a blanket.

"I'll watch whatever you wanna watch."

"Well, how about I don't wanna watch TV," I said while turning the TV off and straddling Luke.

"I'm all for whatever ya sexy ass wants," he said while pulling me in for a kiss.

I know I told y'all I wanted to wait thirty days, but my hot ass lied. When I tell y'all my body had been reacting to this man's every touch. I wanted to jump his bones as soon as we walked in my house. I figured I could at least feed the man first. I started nibbling on his earlobes and inhaling his scent. This man's cologne was so intoxicating. He wore one of my favorite scents, which was Issey Miyake. I stood up and grabbed his hand, pulling him up off the couch. No words were spoken as I led the way to my bedroom. Once we made it to my room, we stood staring at each other for a minute. I started unbuttoning his pants, then I slid them down. After his pants and boxers were down, I pushed him down on my bed and climbed on top. Starting from his forehead, I placed a soft kiss, then went from his cheek to his lips. After placing a million kisses on his face, I ended up on his chest, kissing, licking, and sucking all over him. Before I made it down to his now erect dick, I put my hand down there first to give it a couple of strokes. When I was done stroking him, I ended up face to face with the prettiest dick I'd seen in a long time. Luke was blessed, and I didn't know how I was going to take all of this dick. I kissed the tip of his dick before I took it into my mouth. Looking up at him, I noticed his eyes were closed while he enjoyed the moment.

"Look at me, Luke. I want you to look at me while I'm sucking ya soul out of you," I moaned while swallowing his dick whole.

After deep throating Luke's dick, he shot all his seeds down my throat. While he laid there, savoring the moment, I took all my clothes off. I was so ready to take all of this dick. He pulled me so we were face to face, then he kissed my forehead, then my lips, then he whispered in my ear in a husky tone, "Are you ready for this dick, ma?"

"Yes, I'm ready, baby."

"All right, you know after this, ain't no leaving, beautiful. You're all mine after this." I didn't know whether to be happy or be scared of the way his voice sounded. My body was so ready for him, I forgot how big he was, and that I hadn't done this in a minute. When I hesitated for a second, Luke must have thought something was wrong.

"Are you good, baby? You know we don't have to do this if you're not ready."

"I'm good. We ain't kids and trust me, I've wanted this since the first time I saw you. So, do me a favor and take my body to another place." Once I said that, Luke flipped me over and got on top of me. He started kissing my breasts, making sure to show them both love. He then started kissing my navel, not wasting any time getting down to my honeypot. I guess he was admiring how pretty my kitty was because he stopped for a minute before he dived in. This man was sucking, licking, and kissing on my kitty, causing me to squirm all over the bed. I hadn't had my kitty feasted on for so long. This nigga had a dope-ass head game and a big dick. *Lawd, please let him know how to work that third leg he's carrying around.*

"OH, MY! Luke, I'm cumming," I screamed while creaming all over his face. As soon as I came, Luke looked up at me and smiled, but I guess he wasn't finished down there. He took his thumb and started rubbing it on my clit while he placed two of his other fingers in my opening. While he played with my clit, he continued to move those two fingers in and out of me in a fast motion. Lawd, I didn't know what he was doing or what he was playing with inside of me, but it caused my juices to squirt all over the place. I'd never squirted before, but I'd seen it on Pornhub. Yeah, I watch Pornhub. Don't judge me, a sister has been celibate. After he got done making me cum, he licked his fingers, then kissed my lips.

"You ready for this dick, ma?" He lifted both my legs, threw them on his shoulders and slid into me nice and slow. I tensed up just a little until I adjusted to his size, then Luke dicked me down proper. We ended up exploring each other's body for the rest of the night. Shit, he told me this was going to be it, and I wasn't going anywhere. He had just gained a stalker. I was never letting this dick go.

Kyndall

I was happy when Mom-mom Ella went home, but now I was lonely. It was like everyone had abandoned me. Keem had been acting like I didn't exist in his world, Shawnee had a new boo, and Cash, hell, I didn't know what was up with Cash. I had been calling him all week and hadn't gotten an answer.

Since my man seemed to never be home, I had decided I would cook myself dinner. I hadn't cooked anything in more than a month. Shit, there was no need to since I was always home alone. I just knew that I was good when Mom-mom Ella left. I was getting out of the house and everything, but soon as she was gone, all that ended. It was like I went right back into that depression mode. I didn't want to be alone, but I didn't want to be bothered. The only person I wanted to be around was Cash, and it seemed like he had just kicked me to the curb.

I hadn't showered since Mom-mom Ella was here, so I decided to do that before I headed to the kitchen. I knew my house was probably stinky as hell. It hadn't been cleaned in two weeks. I dragged myself to the bathroom and cut on the shower. I had taken down my sew-in a few days ago, so I desperately needed to wash my hair. Just as I was getting in the shower. I spotted a bottle of wine that I had been drinking on the day before. I walked over to it and downed the whole bottle. I stood there for a second, and that was when it hit me that Cash had pushed me to the side for that thot hoe Nadia.

I headed straight downstairs so I could find my keys. I didn't even worry about cutting the shower off. Cash had me fucked up. I grabbed my purse and the rest of the wine that I had opened this morning and headed to find out what the problem was with Cash.

It took me no time to get to his house since he didn't live far. I parked on his grass and jumped out. I left the car on because I planned on being in and out. I stumbled my way up the stairs. It seemed like he had more stairs than before. When I made it to the door, I had to stop so I could catch my breath. As soon as I felt that I was good, I banged on the door hard as hell. I took a seat on the step and waited, and when no one came, I got up so I could knock again. Just as my hand hit the door, it flew open.

"Why are you beating on my door?" Nadia yelled. I couldn't stand this bitch. She didn't really love Cash, she was with him for his money. I didn't see how he didn't see that.

"Bitch, I'm not here for you. Where is Cash?" I yelled back. Who was she to question me? I was here way before she was.

"Cash is sleep. It's three in the morning."

"Well, let me by so I can wake him up. I need to talk to him, now."

"Look, you are testing me. I suggest you get in your car and find yo' husband or somebody to talk to." I just laughed because she really thought I was going to leave without talking to him. Little did she know, I was the reason he was still with her hoe ass.

"Who the hell is at the door?" I heard Cash yell from behind her. When he made it to the door, for some reason, tears started rolling down my face. I missed him. He had always been there for me, and he hadn't lately, and I didn't know how to cope with that. Shawnee traveled a lot, so it was normal for her not to always answer, but Cash never did that.

"Kyndall, what are you doing here?" he asked me.

"I missed you, and it seemed like everyone just abandoned me. It's normal for Keem and Shawnee, but you have never just left me for dead," I cried. I looked up, and Nadia was looking at me with the stank face. If I had the energy, I would beat her ass.

"Come on, Kyndall. You know I would never do you like that. I have just been busy," he assured me.

"Hell naw. I know damn well you not finna cater to this bitch like I'm not right here. As always, you are putting her before me. How is your relationship going to grow and all you worried about is her?" Nadia yelled. This bitch was really pushing it with me.

"Look, bitch, you have called me out my name too many times. You need to watch your fucking mouth before I beat yo' ass. You need to stay in your lane. I have never stepped on your toes, but you always seem to have something to say about me and Cash's friendship," I finished. I was five seconds from beating her ass.

"Baby, just go upstairs and let me talk to Kyndall for a second," he demanded. She rolled her eyes and walked off.

As soon as she was gone, he pulled me in for a hug, and I felt complete. The feeling that he had just given me, I hadn't ever felt, not even with Keem. At that moment, I realized that I felt something for Cash. It may have been because I was sobering up. Hell, I didn't know what it was.

"What are you doing out this time of morning?"

"I missed you," I cried. I knew I shouldn't be missing him, but I did. He was my husband's best friend, and there was no way I should have been feeling that way.

"I miss you, too," he assured me. When he kissed me on the forehead, I got butterflies in my stomach.

"You don't love me, Cash. No one loves me. My husband doesn't even love me anymore. Like, I don't understand why all of y'all turned y'all back on me. How could y'all just do me like this?" I was crying so hard, I could barely get my words out. I felt so broken. It was like life wasn't worth living anymore. I pulled myself from Cash's arms and headed back to my car. There was no reason for me to be here, especially since Nadia was all that he cared about. I could hear him calling my name, but I just kept moving.

I knew what I needed to do. I was going to make sure none of them had to worry about me ever again.

Chapter eleven

Cash

I stood at my door, shocked. I had seen Kyndall stressed, but never like this. I was worried about her. I tried to catch her, but she had pulled off too fast. I pulled my phone from my pocket and called Keem. I hadn't talked to him much since the day I said something to him about Chrissy.

"What's good? Is everything OK?" he answered. Just then, it hit me that he wasn't at home. If he was, then I knew she wouldn't have been at my house.

"Nigga, you mean to tell me you laid up while yo' wife is having a fucking breakdown," I yelled. I was heated. He was really fucking up. He should have been home, tending to her instead of fucking Chrissy's garbage ass.

"Nigga, my wife at home in the bed. What the hell are you talking about?" he asked me. I wish he were in front of me; I would have beaten his ass. This nigga had the perfect fucking wife, but he would rather be laid up with a thot hoe.

That was one of the things I didn't get about Keem. Kyndall was there when that nigga had nothing, but he treated her like she was the side chick.

"No, your wife just left my house in nothing but a fucking t-shirt and some house shoes. She needs you, and you are nowhere to be found. That shit's not cool, Keem. I know you may be over losing y'all daughter, but she's not. She was drunk as hell. I don't think I've ever seen here like that," I explained. I could hear him moving around, so I was sure he was getting up and getting dressed.

There was nothing more for me to say to him. He was slowly getting on my bad side. I headed to the house so I could put some clothes on and go check on her. As soon as I walked in the door, Nadia was sitting on the couch, looking mad. I really didn't care, though. Kyndall needed me, and there was no way I wasn't going to be there for her. If Nadia didn't like it, then she could simply leave.

"I know you don't think you are going to leave this house and go after her," she said with an attitude. I sighed because she was really pushing it.

"Nadia, don't start that. That's my friend, and I have to make sure she is OK," I explained to her. I was trying to be as nice as possible.

"You need to make a decision. Either it is her or me, but not both. I can't compete with the friendship y'all have, so you are going to have to choose what's more important: your relationship with me or your friendship with her," she said with tears in her eyes. Everything in me said leave and go check on Kyndall, but I went against that and got back in the bed. I just hoped that I didn't regret that decision. When we got back in the bed, Nadia went straight back to sleep. I was happy because she kept talking about Kyndall. It was like she was obsessed with me and Kyndall fucking. That shit was crazy.

I was doing my best to fall back asleep, but I couldn't. The love I had for Kyndall wouldn't let me just leave her out there like that. I knew I wouldn't be able to live with myself if something happened to her. I slowly slid out the bed, hoping I didn't wake Nadia up. I knew she was going to be mad, but I had to check on Kyndall.

Once I was out the bed, I slipped some joggers and a pullover on, then my Nike slides. I grabbed my wallet and keys, then headed out the door. When I pulled into their driveway, a funny feeling came over me. I didn't see Keem's car, but hers was parked sideways by the garage. The door was locked, so I used the spare key they had given me to let myself in.

"Kyndall," I called out. I waited in the living room to see if she was going to say anything. When she didn't reply, I went to their room. As soon as the door opened, I ran to her side, and there was a pill bottle next to her. I checked to see if she was breathing and almost lost it. I knew I should have just told her to stay at my house.

"I knew I shouldn't have let you leave. Baby, please don't leave me," I cried. I hadn't cried in years. To be honest, I think the last time was when my grandfather died. I picked her up and rushed to the car. I wanted to call 911, but I didn't have time to wait; her heartbeat was very faint. I ran every red light getting her to the hospital.

"Help, please," I yelled as I ran into the emergency room with her in my arms. A nurse ran straight over to me.

"What happened?" she asked.

"I don't know. I found her like this." She rushed her straight to the back. I felt lost. I didn't know what to do. I really cared about Nadia, but it was nothing compared to the love I had for Kyndall. For the first time, I saw what everyone else saw. I was indeed in love with Kyndall. I knew I was partially at fault, but if she didn't make it, I was going to kill Hakeem with my bare hands.

While I waited, I called Shawnee but didn't get an answer, so I called Luke. I knew he would answer no matter what time it was.

"What's wrong?" he asked as soon as he answered.

"I need you and Shawnee to get to the hospital, now." He didn't ask any questions, he just ended the call. I wanted to call Keem, but I wanted to see if he would even care enough to look for her, or how long it would take him to call her phone.

Hakeem

The sun shining through the window woke me up out of my sleep. I was extremely tired since I hadn't gotten much sleep, thanks to Cash waking me up out of my sleep. He was fussing about Kyndall's ass like always. I wish he would stay the fuck out of my marriage. I was going to check on her, but since he said she had shown up at his crib, I was like fuck it and climbed back in the bed with Chrissy. I knew I sounded like a fuck nigga right now, but I didn't care. Cash's ass was always on my back about Kyndall's ass. I was starting to believe that he and Kyndall did have some shit going on. Thinking about this shit had me pissed, and ready to get up to take care of my hygiene and check on my wife.

"Baby, where are you going? It's early in the morning. Please come back to bed."

"Chrissy, I have to go. I've been here long enough. Kyndall is starting to get suspicious."

"Keem, do you think I give a damn about how Kyndall feels? She's not the one carrying your baby now, I am." This morning was not the morning, and I didn't feel like dealing with Chrissy's shit.

"Listen, ma, don't start that bullshit. You already know Kyndall is my wife. I already don' fucked up spending too much time with ya ass, now you don't know how to stay in your lane. You may be pregnant, but Kyndall is still Mrs. Richardson."

"You know what, Keem, fuck you. Keep playing with me if you want, and it'll be time for little Mrs. Richardson to know that we're about to be one big happy family."

Hearing her say that angered me. I jumped back in the bed so fast and wrapped my hands around her throat. I blacked out for a second, choking her fucking stupid ass. Her clawing at my face caused me to stop, and I realized I had almost killed the poor girl. Not wanting to say anything else to her, I left her simple ass there to catch her breath and went to take a shower.

Chrissy was starting to get on my damn nerves with her fucking whining and always talking about my wife. I swear she always threw up the fact that Kyndall was not pregnant, and the shit really hurt because it brought back thoughts of Nevaeh. After entering the bathroom, I turned the shower on, then jumped in. While the water was running down my body, thoughts of how my life had become a disaster came to mind. After washing and rinsing a couple of times, I hurried and jumped out. I wrapped my towel around my waist and headed back to Chrissy's room so I could get dressed. She was still lying in bed, crying and sniffling. Not paying her dramatic ass any mind, I headed to the dresser and grabbed my lotion and deodorant, then headed back over to the bed. Mid-step, I started to shake my head. I couldn't believe I had personal items on the dresser, clothes in the closet; hell, I even had a pair of Nike slides next to the bed. My ass had really started doing the most, and that was why Chrissy was the way she was. I felt like a fucking asshole right now. After I finished getting dressed, I slipped my feet into my sneakers, grabbed my phone and my keys, then walked over to Chrissy.

"Baby, stop crying, please. I didn't mean to take my anger out on you. I'm still a little stressed about my daughter dying, and so is Kyndall. You telling her that will kill her, and I don't need that right now. Please just bear with me, and I'll be sure to tell her soon. Let us get over losing our child, Chrissy. Can you please do that for me?" I knew her stupid ass was going to listen to me, but the truth of the matter was that I had no plans of telling my wife anything. I was holding this secret for as long as I could.

"I'm sorry for getting you upset, Keem. I really am, but you know how I feel about you. I'm just so excited to be giving you a baby. I'm sure it will make your life complete." I kissed her forehead and left out the door. I really didn't feel like discussing this anymore. It was bad enough I was on my way home to argue with Unstable Mable. I swear my wife was so fucked up right now, the shit was starting to look like a Lifetime movie.

Chapter twelve

Chrissy

Keem was starting to get on my fucking nerves, always wanting to run to Kyndall's rescue. The little bitch couldn't even give him a baby, but he always worried about her feelings. He never cared about mine. Shit, he leaves here, and sometimes I don't see him for days. Then I have to be reminded that I'm not Mrs. Richardson. Today was the first time he had ever put his hands on me. I thought I was going to die from the way he choked me out.

By the way, my name is Chrissy Delain, and I'm twenty-one years old. Yes, I've been Keem's secretary at his little accountant office. I was supposed to be a temp, but once he got a taste of this good, I became full-time. Yeah, at first, it was just a sex thing to move up in my position at the job. I needed extra money because I was practically homeless, staying in a run-down hotel when I first got to New Jersey. So, my first stop was a temp agency. When I first got the job they assigned and saw Keem's fine ass, I knew I had to work this charm so I could pop this pussy on him. Now look at me in this crazy-ass situation. But guess what? It won't be crazy for long. Keem will be here with me and this baby full time, he just doesn't know it yet.

After lying here in my thoughts, I figured it was time to get my ass up and get dressed. As soon as I was about to go shower, there was a knock at my door. I wasn't expecting anyone, so I wondered who it could be. Once I opened the door, Cash was standing there with an angry scowl on his face.

"So, what do I owe the pleasure of this visit?"

"Where the fuck is Keem's stupid ass?" Cash barked. I stood still for a second, then burst out into a fit of laughter. I couldn't believe he was really at my door.

"Let me guess, his precious Kyndall is looking for him. I wonder what do I have to do to have all these sexy men running to my side? Keem just left to go see what his crybaby-ass Kyndall wants this time." What I said must have struck a nerve because Cash mugged the shit out of me. Hell, I thought my head was going to fly off my shoulders. I didn't think that shit had ever happened to me.

"Listen, you stupid-ass cum sucker, leave Keem the fuck alone. Don't let me have to come over here and tell ya stupid ass again." This asshole was tripping. I couldn't believe he put his hands on me. Being the crazy bitch I am, I looked up at Cash and burst out laughing once again.

"Staying away from Keem gon' be hard to do since I'm carrying his baby." Cash looked at me in disbelief. After I told him my good news, he walked off. You would have thought he was Kyndall's man the way he was acting.

After making sure Cash Dreve off, I shut my door and headed to take a shower. Once I made it to the bathroom, I noticed I had a handprint on my face. I also had Keem's hand prints on my neck. Keem was going to be furious when he finds out the cat is out the bag. Then again, Cash is not going to tell Kyndall; he would rather take that shit to the grave before he hurts Kyndall. I've always thought they had something going on, but I kept it to myself. I felt if Cash kept her occupied, it would give Keem more time with me. After looking at myself once more in the mirror, I adjusted the water temperature, then stepped in.

Hours had past, and I was sitting on the couch, waiting for Keem to at least call me. That didn't happen. Like always, when he goes back home to his wife, he forgets about little old me. I picked up my phone and called him for what seemed like the hundredth time. The phone kept ringing and ringing. Then, of course, the voicemail came on, so I left a nasty-ass message.

"Keep playing with me, Hakeem, and Kyndall will know everything about us tomorrow morning. Now fuck with me if you want to and watch what happens. Don't make it here tonight and you're gonna feel my wrath."After I let Keem know the deal, I threw the phone down with an attitude. Once again, there was a knock at my door, and I swear I wasn't in the mood for any company. When I opened the door, it was my dumb ass brother Dre.

"What the hell you doing here?"

"Come on, sis, don't do me like that. Where's ya dude at?" he asked, looking around the house.

"His stupid ass ain't here. Why, what's up?"

"I wanted to make sure he wasn't here before telling you what I did." Dre and I had a plan to set Keem up, and I had forgotten to stop the deal. See, since I was pregnant, I didn't want to set Keem up anymore. *Fuck man, I hope Dre didn't do any bullshit.*

"What the hell did you do, Dre?" My brother was known to do dumb shit. I hate that I even had Keem to help him get on with Cash.

"I've been stealing money from Cash, and I'ma blame it on ol' boy."

"Dre, I don't wanna set him up no more. I'm pregnant, and we gonna be a family."

"What the fuck, Chrissy? You done got me in some bullshit. Now if this shit backfires, I'm letting the cat out of the bag. Do you really think that nigga gon' stay true to you? He's a fucking married man. The only reason I agreed to do it is because I hate my little sister sitting around here, settling for less when she deserves so much more. I'm done talking to you over and over about this same shit. Our mama didn't raise you to be somebody's side bitch, and when that nigga gets tired of ya stupid ass, don't fucking call me." Dre handed me my ass and stormed out of my house. I hoped to God this shit doesn't bite me in my ass.

Hakeem

I headed straight home because I knew Kyndall would be tripping. Also, I knew nine times out of ten, Cash was here with her, and I didn't want to hear his shit, either. I pulled into the driveway, and her car was here, but I didn't see Cash's car. I headed in the house.

"Kyndall," I called out but didn't get an answer. I knew she was probably in the bed, as always. It seemed that was all she ever did since Nevaeh passed. The only time she left the house was when Ms. Ella was here. Shit, I wish she would have stayed longer because that meant I would have had more time with Chrissy.

After I checked the house, I didn't see her anywhere, so I knew she couldn't be anywhere but at Cash's house. I was seriously starting to think that Nadia was telling the truth. He was more attentive to her than he was to his own bitch. Since I had just thrown on some sweats at Chrissy's house, I decided to put on some clothes. I walked into my closet and pulled out some slacks and a polo shirt since I planned to go to the office today. I had told Chrissy that she could take the day off. It seemed any time she was there, I couldn't get any work done. All she wanted to do was fuck all day. That was how she had ended up pregnant.

I double checked myself in the mirror before I grabbed my keys and headed out the door. When I got to the car, I checked to see if I had a blunt in the glove compartment. Kyndall used to make sure I always had one because I liked to smoke on my way to work. Anger came over me when I realized nothing was there. I started my car and headed straight to Cash's house. Kyndall was going to have to get her shit in line and fast. I understood she was hurt, but this was not the first time that we had lost a baby. She should have expected this shit to happen.

When I pulled in Cash's gate, I didn't see his car, which was weird since I knew there was no way Cash had left Nadia and Kyndall here together. They hated each other, so I knew that wasn't the case.

I knocked on the door a few times, and when I didn't get an answer, I pulled out my keys. I had a key to their house, but I didn't use it unless I needed to.

I walked into the house, and Kevin Gates was blasting. I knew that meant Nadia was in here. There was no way Kyndall would be caught listening to rap. She hated it. Just thinking about that brought back memories of our first date. I had picked her up, and I was blasting NWA. She stood outside of the car until I cut it off. She said that I wasn't going to poison her mind. I laughed to myself as I walked through the house. I followed the music until I made it to Cash's bedroom.

Nadia was dancing in the mirror, ass naked. That shit had my dick hard as fuck. It was damn near busting through my pants. She was so into the music that she didn't see me standing there, so I decided to scare her ass. I pulled my slacks down and walked up behind her. As soon as I was close, I pushed her over on the chaise that was next to the mirror. Before she had a chance to scream, I slid my dick into her, then kissed her on the neck.

"Damn, I miss this pussy," I moaned. I was sure she realized who I was at that point because she started throwing that ass back. Shit, I now knew why Cash still fucked with her: she had some bomb-ass pussy.

"What are you doing here?" she managed to get out.

"Looking for Cash and Kyndall. She wasn't at home, so I thought she was over here," I replied, not missing a stroke. I used my leg to push the chaise in front of the mirror. I wanted to look at her while I fucked her. As soon as I had a good view, I went in. I knew that after today, she would be acting just like Chrissy. This was going to be my pussy from this day forward.

After two hours and three nuts, I was laying in their bed, ass naked. I looked over at the nightstand, and my eyes landed on a picture of me Cash and Kydall at our high school graduation. Seeing that picture made me feel bad as hell. I had broken the ultimate bro code. I had fucked my best friend's bitch in his house and bed.

"Why are you looking like that? What's done is done now," Nadia said, pulling me from my thoughts. That told me she knew what we had done wasn't cool.

"I'm not dumb. I know that what we did is done, but that doesn't make the shit cool."

"Well, I figured since they fucking, so should we. That dick you gave me last time was good, but today was the fucking bomb. Shit, I see why she married yo' ass."

"Nadia, shut the fuck up, I'm thinking," I yelled. I was trying to get my thoughts together, and she was talking. I hated that shit.

I sat on the end of the bed and tried to figure out where in the hell they could be. I pulled my phone out and called Kyndall's phone. She didn't answer, so I called Cash.

"Yea?"

"Where is Kyndall?" I asked. I knew he was going to get mad, but I didn't care at this moment. There was no reason they should have been anywhere together. She should have been home.

"Where the fuck are you? While you were laid up with that hoe Chrissy, your wife almost killed herself. If you had been at home rather than at Chrissy's house, you would have known that." Hearing what he said knocked the wind out of my body. How could she do something like that?

I jumped up and threw my clothes back on and headed out. I didn't worry about saying anything to Nadia. I ran to my car and headed straight to the hospital. How could he not call me and tell me what was going on with her?

I parked in the first spot I could find and headed to see my wife. I knew she was going to be pissed, but she would get over it. Hell, it was her fault.

I walked to the desk to see where she was. I knew Cash probably wasn't going to answer for me, so I didn't bother calling. As soon as the lady told me what room she was in, I headed straight to her side. When I walked into the room, my knees went weak; she was hooked up to all kinds of shit. How could I not be there for her? I guess I was so into Chrissy and the fact that I was finally going to be a father, I had pushed my wife to the back of my mind, and look where that got me. I just prayed that she pulled through.

Chapter Thirteen

Shawnee

I couldn't believe Kyndall had tried to kill herself. I partially blamed myself because I really hadn't been going to check on her, or even calling. I knew how depressed she was, but I put her on the back burner for Luke.

"Baby, stop crying," Luke begged as he rubbed my back. We were sitting in the waiting area, praying the doctor delivered some good news.

"I just don't know what I would do if I lost her," I cried.

"You are not going to lose her, baby. She is way stronger than y'all are giving her credit for," he assured me. I looked over to the other side of the room, and it was like Cash was in a daze. When we first got here, he told us that she had come to his house and he sent her back home, so I was more than sure his head was in a fucked up place.

I was getting ready to go over and check on Cash, but the doctor came out.

"Family of Kyndall Richardson." We all jumped up and headed towards him. He ushered us into a family room, which made me think that things were really bad.

"Are you all kin to her? We aren't allowed to disclose patient information with anyone outside of the family," the doctor asked Cash as soon as we walked in the room. That made me think about the fact that Keem wasn't here. I made a mental note to call as soon as we got done. This was the second time he hadn't made my friend a priority.

"Yes, I'm her brother, and that's her sister," Cash mumbled.

"It's good that you found her when you did. She took several meds that shouldn't be mixed together. We have her in a medically induced coma right now. The mixture of drugs nearly stopped her heart. Right now, she can't breathe on her own, but we hope that she will be able to in the near future. She is blessed. It's a miracle that she is still with us."

I felt like I was going to die. There was no way this could really be happening. How could she do this? All she had to do was call me. I would've stopped what I was doing just to see about her. After we finished talking to the doctor, I called Mom-mom Ella. I knew she was going to be pissed because she had told me to make sure I checked on her every day. I ended the call with her, and we headed to the room Kyn was assigned to. As soon as I laid eyes on her, I wanted to cry. She was hooked up to all kinds of machines. It took everything in me to hold it together.

"Cash, what made her do this?" I asked. When I looked over at him, tears were rolling down his face. That was the first time I had ever seen him cry.

"I don't know. I should have just taken her home myself," he mumbled. He blamed himself, and that was not cool. We were all at fault, especially Hakeem. We sat there in silence for nearly two hours. All that could be heard were sniffles.

"Where the fuck is that bitch-ass husband of hers?" Mom-mom Ella said, making her presence known. I knew she was going to be the one to question why he wasn't here. She never really liked him, she just dealt with him because Kyndall loved him.

"I don't know, but I'm going to find him," Cash said as he walked out the room. Luke followed behind, leaving Mom-mom Ella and me there.

"I'm going to assume that you hadn't been by to check on her like I told you. I knew I should have stayed with her. Hell, his ass was gone the whole time I was there. I told him she didn't need to be alone."

"No, I hadn't." I felt like a child under Mom-mom Ella's eyes. I knew she was disappointed in me.

"Listen to me. God has the last say so. It's not over until He says it's over. She's a fighter," she told me as she rubbed my back. I was strong, but if I lost Kyndall, I would be no more good.

 Kyndall and I had practically grown up with Mom-mom Ella, being as though my parents were drug addicts, and Kyndall's parents cared more about work than her. Mom-mom Ella came in and stepped up to the plate, and I must say, she raised us well all alone.

I remember on the first day of school, Kyndall stood up for me when this guy was picking on me. I knew how to defend myself, but I was in a new environment, and that shit scared the hell out of me. It seemed that I didn't fit in, and talked and dressed differently. Kyndall didn't care about any of that; we were cousins, and we loved each other.

I went through that my whole ninth grade year since all of the clothes I had were old clothes my mom had gotten from Goodwill. Most of them were too big, and all of the shoes were too little. I looked like a straight junky. That was where I got the passion for making clothes. I told Mom-mom Ella that I wanted to make my own clothes.

"Look, stop thinking she is gone. She can hear you. Now get it together," she damn near yelled. I wanted to curse her old ass out, but I knew better. She didn't play. I tried to talk back when I first moved with her, and she beat my ass something serious. I made a vow that I would never try her again. We sat and talked about old times until Cash and Luke walked back in the door.

"We couldn't find him." Cash looked so defeated. I knew he was going to click the moment Keem showed his face. Mom-mom looked at Cash and went over to hug him. This was really weighing on him.

"Well, just call me if y'all need me. I will try and come by after church tomorrow night," Mom-mom said before she headed out. Luke walked her downstairs, and Cash took her seat next to Kyndall. Just as I was about to sit down, Cash's phone rang. I knew by the way he answered that it was Keem calling. Shortly after they ended the call, Keem walked into the room, looking like he was really concerned. If you didn't know him, you would have really thought he cared by the look on his face.

"Well, look who decided to show his face."

"Shawnee, I'm not for your bullshit today. I'm here to check on my wife," Keem said with an attitude. I was happy that Luke wasn't in here because he would have beaten his ass.

"Watch yo' fucking mouth," Cash yelled. I knew shit was about to get ugly. Cash looked like he was the fucking devil.

"When it comes to my wife, I can say and do what I want," Keem yelled back.

"You can stop pretending that you give a fuck. She could have died. You should have been there for her, but you were too busy fucking that hoe who works for you. How can you do her like that? She loves you damn near more than she loves herself and you dogging her out like she some freak hoe. That shit ain't cool," Cash stated, walking toward Keem. I didn't know why Keem wanted to play with Cash. He knew better than that.

"How can you tell me how I feel? You just mad she's my wife and not yours—" Before Hakeem could finish his sentence, Cash started throwing blows on his ass. I wanted to laugh, but I knew it wasn't the time. Luke walked in just in time to break them up before security came. I was happy because I knew he would have told them he didn't want us here.

"You a real fuck nigga. You dead to me. I can't wait till she leaves yo' ass when she finds out that you got another bitch pregnant," Cash yelled as Luke held him back.

"What did you just say?" I asked to be sure that I had heard the right thing. I knew my ears had to be playing tricks on me. There was no way he was doing my girl that bad.

"Tell her, Hakeem." Cash was pissed. This was so out of character for him. He would never put anyone's business out like that, especially if he knew it could hurt Kyndall. I know they say they can still hear when they're in a coma, I just hoped she was an exception to the rule.

"Stay out of my business," was all Keem said before walking out the door. Once again, he was being the same selfish Hakeem and putting her needs last. He was really showing his true colors. I knew that whenever Kyndall woke up, all hell was going to break loose.

Nadia

After Keem ran out the door like a crazy person, I hurried and jumped up, changed my sheets and headed for the shower before Cash came strolling in. I had even lit my Bath & Body Works candle to get rid of the sex smell. I couldn't believe I had just fucked in my man's bed. What the fuck was wrong with me? Usually, I didn't feel any type of way when I was fucking with another nigga, but the fact that I had done it in our bed made me feel like shit. I hopped in the shower and took care of my hygiene, then jumped out. Once I slipped on my grandmom pajamas, I headed downstairs to cook dinner for Cash and I. I knew he would probably ask why I had changed the sheets, and the first thing that came to mind was my period came on. I knew he would believe me because of what I was wearing. When I made it downstairs, Cash was already sitting in the living room in his own thoughts. I walked over to him and climbed into his lap.

"Hey, baby. Why didn't you call to let me know you were here?" I asked. He didn't answer me, he didn't even look my way. I looked into his eyes, and I could see the hurt.

"Cash, baby, what's wrong?"

"I wasn't there for her like I should have been. My best friend needed me, and I pushed her away because of you," he yelled while pushing me off his lap. I hit the floor hard as hell, and he got up and walked off like he hadn't just thrown me, his girlfriend, on the floor. I jumped up so fast and headed right up the steps behind his simple ass.

"You know what, Cash? You are not gonna be disrespectful to me over that bitch." Why did I say that shit? He came running at me like a raging bull and grabbed me by my neck.

"Nadia, don't you ever call her out of her name again. Do you fucking hear me?" I couldn't speak, so all I did was nod my head. When he got the answer he wanted, he let my ass go, and I fell on the floor, gasping for air. The tears started running down my face instantly. If I didn't know it before, I definitely knew it now: this nigga really loves Kyndall. I got up off the floor, wiped my face then headed to put some clothes on. I would not be staying in this house with his crazy ass. After I put my clothes on, I grabbed a duffel bag out the closet and packed a couple of outfits. I didn't plan on coming back for a couple of days. I could see Cash needed some time to himself, and I would give him his space. Once I grabbed everything I needed to last me a couple of days, I nearly ran out the front door, not looking back. When I made it to my car, I pulled my phone out and shot Keem a text.

Me: Hey, you. I can use some company.

Keem: Me too. I'll meet you where we first met up.

Me: Cool, I'm headed there right now.

My feelings were a little hurt, but I knew Keem would keep my mind off of what was going on. Fifteen minutes went by, and I was pulling up to the hotel. Once I parked, I texted Keem to let him know I was here, and he sent me the room number. Then he told me to tell them the room and they would give me a key. After I grabbed my bag and purse, I headed in the hotel. To be honest with y'all, I just wanted to be held for the night. This shit with Cash really had me in my feelings. When I entered the hotel, I walked straight over to the desk and asked for the key. Once I had it, I headed for the elevator. The elevator ride seemed to take forever. Just as I was about to get off, Dre was stepping on with this beautiful chick. When I tell y'all my blood was boiling. He gave me a strange look, I guess not wanting me to say shit, but I didn't give a fuck. Petty Betty was one of my names so it wouldn't be me if I didn't say anything.

"Well, hello, Dre. Long time no see. Are you gonna introduce me to your friend?"

"Hey, Nadia. What's good, ma? Reneé, this is Nadia, my boss' girl."

"Well, hello, Nadia, it's nice to meet you. Maybe we can get together and double date sometimes, Dre." I wasn't sure what was going on, and who his boss was, but I was going to try my luck.

"Wait, Cash is ya boss, Dre? I never knew that."

"Yes, he's been my boss for years. I find that hard to believe that you didn't know. Well, this is my stop. Let me and my wife go enjoy our anniversary, and I'll find out when the next time Cash is free so we can do a date night." Hearing him say his wife made my mouth hit the floor. I wondered how long he had known Cash was my man. Today was just too much, and I couldn't wait to get in this room to shower, then go to bed. I'd been cheating to get back at Cash, and these niggas stayed one-upping me. I couldn't do shit but shake my head at the thought of Dre being married.

Chapter fourteen

Luke

It had been a couple of days since the shit had happened with Kyndall, and Shawnee had been a fucking mess. Baby girl didn't want to eat, get dressed, wash her ass or anything. She hadn't been answering my phone calls all night long. Cash had just called me and told me she hadn't come up to the hospital all day, so I went by Mom-mom Ella's house to see if she had a spare key to Shawnee's crib because I knew if I just showed up, she wasn't going to let me in. Mom-mom Ella gave me a hard time at first, so I had to get Cash to call and talk to her. I see how much she loved Cash, and I hoped she'd get to like me that way in the future because I would hate to be on her bad side. That was a mean-ass old lady, but I see the way she loves Shawnee and Kyndall like she had given birth to them.

After a long-ass forty-five minutes of trying to get the key, I was finally pulling up to Shawnee's crib. Once I parked the car, I jumped out and headed up to her door. I knocked first, but after knocking on the door hard as hell, I still didn't get an answer, so I pulled the key out and let myself in. When I made it in the house, I could see Shawnee lying on the couch from the front door. There was an empty Crown Royal bottle and an empty wine bottle. Shawnee was on the couch with just a dingy t-shirt and a pair of panties on. All I could do was shake my head at her crazy ass. She always tried to put on this strong persona, but sometimes, the strongest people need a shoulder to lean on. Leaving her on the couch, I walked upstairs to her bathroom to run her a bubble bath. I turned the water on, then checked the closet for some bubble bath. I was moving so fast, and something fell on the floor. Looking down to see what it was, I noticed it was a dildo. I picked it up and threw it right in the trash. *She will no longer need it,* I said to myself. Once I put the bubbles in the water, I headed back downstairs to get her while the water ran. I picked her up bridal style, and she didn't budge until I kissed her forehead.

"Luke, what are you doing here?" she slurred.

"I'm here to take care of you, baby. When's the last time you ate?" She giggled and put her head on my shoulder. I knew right then and there she was still drunk. When we made it to the bathroom, I sat her down in the vanity chair and helped her out of her clothes. Once her shirt was off, she pulled me in for a hug. My dick bricked up instantly, but I knew this wasn't the time.

"Luke, I want you to fuck me."

"Not right now, baby. We need to get you cleaned and get you something to eat."

"OK. My head is hurting, Luke."

"I bet it is. Why were you drinking like that?"

"I don't know. I guess I was in my feelings."

"Why weren't you answering me last night? I would have come over here and stayed with you, Shawnee. I get that you wanna be strong all the time, and you blame yourself for not being there for Kyndall, but, baby, you can't save the world. You have been there time and time again for Kyndall, but because you weren't this time doesn't mean you have to blame yourself. It's not your fault she's laying in that hospital bed. Keem's sorry ass is the reason, so please stop blaming yourself. Shawnee, I don't take being pushed away too well, so if you don't want a nigga to be around just let me know and I'll keep it moving."

"Luke, I'm sorry, and of course, I want you around."

"Well, don't ever ignore me like that again. Had me getting cursed out by Mom-mom Ella for trying to get your key to get in here. Now, come on, let's get in the bath."

After Shawnee was in the tub, relaxing, I headed downstairs to see what she had to cook. My ass was starving, and I knew she probably was, too. Looking in her fridge, her ass had all healthy looking shit. Don't get me wrong, I believed in good health, but I wanted some wings, a cheesesteak, and some cheese fries. I pulled out my phone, called Temples Pizza, and ordered everything I wanted, then I headed in the living room while I waited for the food and Shawnee to get done.

A loud knock at the door woke me up out of my sleep. I jumped up and went to answer the door, and it was the delivery guy. After I paid the dude, I grabbed the food and headed to the kitchen. I looked down at my phone and noticed that Shawnee had been upstairs for about forty-five minutes now, so I figured I would head up there and see what she was doing. When I made it to the bathroom, she wasn't in there, so I went to her room. The sight before me had me wanting to climb in the bed with her, but I decided against it. My stomach grumbling brought me out of my thoughts, reminding me that I had food downstairs. I let her sleep while I went to eat. Once I was finished eating, I decided to go upstairs and climb right in the bed behind her.

Cash

The shit with Kyndall had a nigga all fucked up. I didn't think I'd ever cried this much in my whole life. Every day, I'd been going by, checking on Kyndall. I hadn't seen Keem since we fought in the hospital a couple of days ago. I'd been checking the visitor's list, and I noticed he hadn't been here. I noticed Shawnee hadn't come up, so I called Luke to see if he had talked to her. When he told me no, and said he was going to check on her, I was cool with that. I also hadn't seen Nadia in a couple of days, since she had stormed out of my crib. After she left, I was mad as hell at myself because I had treated her badly. I'd been calling her, but she hadn't answered me. I knew she was mad, and I felt fucked up for how I had treated her, but it was time for her to bring her little ass home.

Me: I know you're mad, and I'm sorry, Nadia.

Nadia: You hurt my feelings, Cash.

Me: I know, ma, and I promise you I'm sorry.

Nadia: You love Kyndall, and I can't compete with that. I think it's a good idea if I give you your space.

Me: Ma, I don't want my space, I want you. Meet me at the house tonight so we can talk.

Nadia didn't respond, but knowing her, she would be there with bells on. I did my morning visit with Kyndall, and when I was finished talking to her, I kissed her forehead and headed out. Luke and I were going to meet up with the accountant who had taken over Keem's job. I needed to know who was robbing me. I shot Luke a text, telling him to meet me at the spot. A half hour had passed, and Luke was pulling up the same time I was.

"What's good, bro?"

"Nothing much, just tired as hell. How's Kyndall doing?"

"She's still the same, bro. How's Shawnee doing?"

"Man, she is going through it, blaming herself for what went down. I keep trying to explain to her that it's not her fault. You know it's not ya fault, either, bro. The one who is responsible for this is her bitch-ass husband." No matter how much everyone told me it wasn't my fault, I just wouldn't let myself believe it. If I had just taken her home or made her stay in one of my guest rooms, she would have been fine.

"I don't wanna talk about this shit, man. Can we just go inside and handle this business? Where is your man at? Why isn't he here yet?"

"Calm down, Cash, he is on his way." I knew my attitude was on one right now, and to be honest, I didn't need to be doing this right now.

"My fault, man. I'm still going through something."

"You need to be home relaxing and laying up under ya girl."

"Man, I think I fucked up with Nadia."

"What happened, Cash?"

"The day I left the hospital, I blamed her for this happening to Kyndall. See, Kyndall had stopped by earlier that day, all fucked up, and I kind of brushed her off, so when I got home, I went off on Nadia."

"Damn yo, that's crazy."

"That's not even all of it. You know how Nadia can't stand me and Kyndall's friendship, so we both said some hateful things to each other, but when she called Kyndall a bitch, I choked her up."

"Cash, what the fuck, man? You trippin. We don't put our hands on females; we leave first, bro. Yeah, lil sis got you gone. Ain't no way in hell y'all two don't love each other in more than a friendship way. You can say it ain't like that all you want, but I damn sure ain't buying it. Come on, let's go in; here come dude now." I was so into the conversation, I hadn't even heard homeboy walk up. Yeah, my ass was not even checking out my surroundings. Kyndall really did have my head gone. We all entered the building where I held my meetings. I didn't know this weird-ass looking dude, but if he was cool with Luke, he was fine with me.

"So, what did you find, my man?"

"Well, from the numbers I was given, shit definitely not adding up. Somebody has been robbing you for a couple of months now, and looking deeper into everything, as far as drops, I've noticed that someone has been pinching off of each Drep. The reason you haven't noticed is because they wait until you do that final count." Luke was furious as hell. He looked madder than me.

"Nobody has access to the drops but Keem's bitch ass," Luke snapped. I didn't want to believe this shit, but with the fucking shit Keem had been doing, I didn't put shit past his stupid ass.

"All right, homie, thanks for all your help. Luke, pay him so he can go." Luke pulled out a yellow envelope full of money and handed it to ol' dude, then he walked him out.

"So, how we gon' handle this?" Luke asked, walking back in.

"Man, I have no idea, but for the time being, let's not do anything. I want to catch his bitch ass in action."

"All right, bro, cool. I'm gon' head out. I slipped out while Shawnee was sleeping. Hopefully, when I get back, she's still asleep, so I can slip back in bed with her." After we dapped each other up, he went his way, and I went mine. I was headed home with hopes that Nadia was there or on her way.

■■

After taking a much-needed shower, I was headed back to my room. I was so ready to get in my bed and relax. Usually, I would go see Kyndall before I turned in for the night, but today, I just didn't feel like it. I'd go to see her first thing in the morning like I did every day before I started my day. Once I made it in my room, Nadia sitting on my bed brought a smile to my face.

"Hey, you. I was wondering how much longer you were going to take in there."

"My fault, ma. If I had known you were coming, I would have cut it short. Let me put some ballers on, then we can talk." I walked over to my dresser and grabbed my shorts out of the drawer, then I slipped them on. After I was comfortable, I grabbed Nadia's hand and led her downstairs to the living room.

"I'm so sorry about the other night, and I completely understand if you don't ever wanna speak to me."

"I accept your apology, Cash, but I still don't think I have it in me to compete with Kyndall."

"Nadia, I swear to you, Kyndall and I don't have anything going on. I feel like if you get to know her and act cordial around her, then you would feel differently about her. As long as we've been together, you haven't given her a chance."

"I guess you're right, so how about I'll try for you, and you try to make our relationship work. Cash, I shouldn't feel like I'm the friend and she's the wifey. If you can't change just a little with y'all friendship, then leave me alone." The situation that had happened the other night was really fucked up, and the least I could do at this very moment was agree with Nadia on trying to change.

Chapter Fifteen

Kyndall

I didn't know what the hell was going on, but I couldn't wake up for the life of me. It seemed that I had slept forever. I could hear voices, but I couldn't make out everything they were saying. The only way I could understand the voices was when they were close. The voice I heard the most was Cash's, but one voice I didn't hear often was Keem's. I even heard Luke and Mom-mom Ella.

I couldn't take being asleep anymore, so I fought as hard as I could to open my eyes. When I finally did, Cash was right next to me with his back turned. I knew that it was him because of all that damn hair.

"Oh my God, she's up," Shawnee cried. She rushed over while Luke walked out the room. I guess he had gone to get the doctor because he walked in shortly after Luke walked out. My throat was dry as hell. I guess Cash had read my mind because he brought me a cup of water. I watched as the doctor moved around the room. He checked my vitals and went on about his way.

"I'm so happy you awake, baby," Cash whispered in my ear. *Did he just call me baby?* I just brushed it off because he probably hadn't meant to say that.

"How long have I been asleep?"

"Two weeks," Cash told me. "But you up now, and that's all that matters to me," he smiled. For some reason, I got butterflies. All I could do was stare at him. He was so handsome. Shit, I shouldn't have been looking at him like that.

"Girl, if you ever do some dumb shit like that again, I will kill you myself," Shawnee fussed, causing me to break the stare off that was going on between Cash and me. I knew that what I had done was stupid, but it was done now. I couldn't change it or take it back.

"Sorry," I mumbled. When I attempted to kill myself, I didn't think about how it would affect them. I knew they loved me, but I was so hurt. All I could think about was being with my baby.

"Where is Keem?" I asked. I could tell that something was wrong. No one said anything, and that said everything I needed to know.

"Do you want me to call him?" Cash asked. I shook my head no. I knew I hadn't heard his voice, but I wanted to see if he would come and check on me.

"Has he even been here? I could hear y'all, but I hadn't really heard his voice. When I was sleep, I could hear everything y'all were saying." Cash looked at me with sadness in his eyes.

"Look, I don't know where the fuck Keem could be. He has come by a few times, but none of us were here when he came," Shawnee explained. I knew Cash didn't want to tell me that. Shawnee was still talking, but I couldn't make out what she was saying. I could feel the tears building in my eyes. *How could he not check on me? Did he not love me anymore?*

I looked over at Cash, and he rushed to my side, and that was when everything came back to me. The reason I had done this was because he didn't want to see me. "Cash, do you love her more than you love me?" The whole room got quiet. I was sure they didn't expect me to ask that. The truth was, I didn't think I could handle the answer, but I wanted to know.

"Kyndall, she is my girl, but you know I love you. There's no question about that." I knew what that meant. I turned my head to face the wall. I didn't want them to see the tears that were streaming down my face. I wish I could just run away.

"Give us a minute, y'all," I heard Cash say from behind me. Shortly after, I heard the door close.

"Kyndall, you know I love you, but I have to put my relationship first. You have a husband—"

"Who doesn't care enough about me to come and see if I'm dead or alive," I finished his sentence.

"It's OK, Cash,' I tried assuring him. I knew he wouldn't go for it, but I took my chance. I made up in my mind right then that I was done with Cash and Keem. Cash had Nadia, and I didn't want to be the one to come in between that. Who knew who Keem had, but clearly, they were way more important than me.

"Kyndall, baby, look, I just don't know what to say."

"Stop calling me that. You can go and tell Shawnee that I just need some time alone." I didn't want to be a burden on any of them. I knew he wanted to say something, but he didn't, he just left the room.

I waited for a few minutes, then I called the doctor in the room. It took a while, but he finally came.

"Good evening, Mrs. Richardson. You called for me?"

"How soon can I get out of here?"

"I will check to see and let you know in an hour or so," he told me.

"I don't want any visitors. If I can't go home, can you move me to another room and make sure I'm not in the directory?" I added. I didn't want to be found. I needed to focus on myself and getting better.

"No problem," was all he said before leaving the room. Once he was gone, I reached for my phone. I called Sprint and had my number changed. I didn't want to be bothered.

After all of that was done, I just laid in the bed, thinking about what I could do to get my life back in line. I knew it was going to take a lot to get my life in order, but I had to do what I had to do.

An hour and a half later, the doctor came in and told me that I would be able to go home the next day after they did some testing. That was all I needed to hear.

■■

****

It had been nearly a week since I was discharged from the hospital. I had been staying at the Hyatt place in Mt. Laurel, NJ. I had even gone as far as booking the room under a fake name. I knew Cash had the resources to find me if I would have booked it under my name. Hell, he might not even be looking for me, but I just wanted to be sure that if he did, he wouldn't be able to find me.

I couldn't lie and say that I didn't miss Cash. Even though I couldn't respond, I loved to hear him talk to me and tell me how much he loved me. That was something Keem never did, even when we were good.

I knew I was making a bad decision, but I decided to call his phone. I just wanted to hear his voice.

"Hello?" His voice relaxed me, just like that.

"Kyndall, is that you?" *How the hell did he know it was me?* He wasn't supposed to know that. I didn't need to make that call because I knew that if he would have spoken one more word, then I would have given in to him. I knew Cash would trace the call, so I packed up my things so I could check out and find another hotel a little further away.

After I checked out, I headed to the Borgata Hotel and Casino in Atlantic City. As soon as I made it there, I powered my cell off and got into bed. I wanted to sleep, but I knew that wasn't going to happen. Once my head hit the pillow, tears started rolling. My life was a mess. I wondered if Keem was looking for me. I missed him. I missed the love we once shared. I wanted that back. I wanted my husband to love me like he used to.

Hakeem

I just knew that Nadia was trying to get some attention the day she told me that Cash and Kyndall had something going on. Shit, now I believed her ass. There had to be something going on between them. Hell, he was riding harder for her than I was, and I was her husband. I knew he cared for her, but he was ready to go to war with me about her like she was his wife. That shit had been heavy on my mind. I wanted to ask him about it, but I know that would just make a bigger issue than we already had.

Since I hadn't been to see Kyndall in over a week, I decided I would go. I really didn't like seeing her like that, but she was my wife.

"Baby, I will be back later," I yelled to Chrissy. I had been living with her since Kyndall had been in the hospital. I knew I should have been staying at the hospital with her, but she wouldn't know if I was there or not, so I would lie and tell her I had been there.

"OK, baby. I'm going to the office so I can get some work done. Call me and let me know when you headed back this way so I can have dinner ready," she yelled back. I couldn't front and say that I wasn't enjoying Chrissy. I was actually happy, but I knew that she could never be Kyndall. She could cook, but it was nothing like Kyndall's food. My wife could throw down in the kitchen. Damn, I missed Kyndall's ass.

I slipped my shoes on, then headed to kiss Chrissy goodbye. On the way to the car, my phone rang. I saw that it was an unknown number, so I hit ignore. I knew it was probably Nadia calling. We had been meeting almost every day. I made a mental note to call her when I was done with Kyndall. Never in a million years would I have thought that I would be fucking my best friend's bitch. I told myself that I was going to be done after the second time, but that went out the window.

The ride to the hospital wasn't long because Chrissy didn't live far. I parked in the first parking spot I could find. When I walked in, I told the lady at the desk who I was there to see, and to my surprise, she said they didn't have a patient by that name. I knew damn well she hadn't passed and no one had called me. I thanked the lady and headed back to my car. I pulled out my phone and decided to give Cash a call. Once I dialed his number, he picked up on the first ring.

"Yea?" Cash answered.

"I just came to see Kyndall, and they said she's not here. What the hell is going on?" I questioned.

"She's your wife, not mine," was all he said before ending the call. I didn't know what had been going on with him lately. The only dealings we had was business, and that had even been slow. I just brushed it off and headed to my office so I could check on Chrissy.

"Hey, baby. I didn't expect to see you here." Something was off about her. Normally, she would be all over me.

"I got done sooner than I expected," I said as I walked past her into my office. Once I was in my office, and the door was closed, I called Kyndall's phone number. It was disconnected. That was weird. I then called Shawnee so I could see if she had talked to her. They never went without talking.

"Why are you calling my phone? I hope you have found her. If not, get the fuck off my phone."

I had to look at the phone because I knew damn well she wasn't talking to me, and what the hell was she talking about, found her? Where the hell was she?

"What you talking about, find her?"

"Nigga, get the fuck off my phone." I guess since she was fucking with Luke, she had found her voice.

I took a seat, so I could gather my thoughts. I felt like shit. My wife was missing, and I was laid up, fucking my side bitch. I had really lost myself. This was not like me at all. Kyndall was my first everything. How could I treat her that way? I had my head laid back, thinking until I felt my zipper being unzipped. I looked down, and Chrissy was on her knees with my whole dick in her mouth. That shit felt so good, all thoughts of Kyndall were gone.

Chapter sixteen

Chrissy

I didn't expect Keem to come to the office. I had been trying my best to hide the fact that I was looking for Cash's file so I could see where his money was going. I noticed that I hadn't really been seeing any transactions. I really didn't want to help my brother, but I didn't really have a choice. I knew that he would tell Cash and put it all on me. My brother didn't have love for anyone but his hoe-ass wife. I hated her. She was the one who had turned him against me.

I knew I couldn't tell him what was going on because Cash already hated me. I wish I wouldn't have told him I was pregnant. Keem damn near beat my ass when he found out that I had told Cash. I knew Cash wasn't going to tell Kyndall, but he didn't believe me.

After he was in his office, I fixed all the files back how they were, then I headed to his office to distract him. He loved when I sucked his dick when he had a lot on his mind. He said that it helped him think.

"Shit, baby. Rub them balls," he demanded. I did what I was told. I knew that he would be nutting soon. My fucking neck was hurting. I had been sucking his dick for almost an hour. That had never happened. It seemed he wasn't into it today. After he nutted down my throat, I cleaned my face and then headed to fix him some coffee.

As I was walking down the hallway, I could hear him on the phone. I guess it was Cash because they were talking about Kyndall. I heard him say that she was missing. I swear that shit gave me a reality check. I knew that he wouldn't give a damn about me if he didn't care about his wife.

"Here's your coffee," I said as I walked back in his office. He just nodded. I guess Cash had hung up because he threw his phone at the wall. That was my cue to get away from him. He needed his space. I was walking out the door when I felt hot liquid. I wanted to scream. I knew that was going to leave a mark on my yellow skin.

"Why the fuck did you bring me that cold-ass coffee? Go and make me some more," he yelled. It took everything in me not to cry. He hadn't ever treated me like that. I headed back to the kitchen so I could fix him some more. After I brewed a new pot, I fixed him a cup and took it to him.

"Go home and cook me something to eat," he yelled. I hurried out the door; I didn't want him to throw that one at me, too. Once I was in the car, I let the tears roll. I felt like I was going backward in my life rather than forward. My phone rang, and I saw it was him. I wanted to ignore his call, but I knew he would really act crazy.

"Hello?"

"If I find out you on some fuck shit, I'm going to kill you, and we both know no one will miss you."

I just held the phone. All I could do was cry because what he had said was true. After he hung up, I headed home so I could cook and get the house clean. I didn't need him going off on me again.

Nadia

Things had been every bit of amazing until that fucking Kyndall woke up. Cash and I had gotten back on good terms, and we were loving on one another like crazy. Even when Kyndall woke up, he was still Team Nadia. Shit, it was getting harder and harder for me to go see Keem and answer Dre's phone calls since Cash was all in my face. I was loving every bit of it. Then, here comes Kyndall again. Apparently, her ass is missing, and no one knows where she is, and Cash has been in the streets day in and day out, looking for her miserable ass. To be honest, I was hoping they didn't find her crazy ass. The minute I stood up, I got light headed and almost fell, but Cash caught me. I didn't even know he had walked into the room.

"Damn baby, you good?"

"Yes, I'm good, just felt a little dizzy. I'll be OK. Just let me sit down for a second." I was about to sit down, but I felt like I needed to vomit, so I ran to the bathroom. Now I was standing over the toilet, throwing up everything I had eaten today while Cash was holding my hair, and rubbing my back.

"You good, ma?" he said in a confused tone. Shit, I was just as shocked as he was because I never got sick.

"I don't know where that came from. Maybe I have food poisoning or the flu."

"Or maybe you pregnant. We have been fucking like rabbits around here since you've been back home." Cash wasn't lying, but the problem with that was, he wasn't the only person I was fucking. This just couldn't be my life right now.

"I don't think so, Cash."

"Nadia, I know when you are bleeding. Whenever your period is here, you are one evil-ass woman, and we argue like crazy. Lately, we haven't been arguing. Not to mention, you haven't come to bed in those granny pajamas in a minute. You have been bringing that ass to bed naked." It had been so much shit going on, I hadn't even realized I hadn't had my period. I guess Cash paid more attention to me than I thought.

"Well, I guess you're right, baby. We can go to the doctor tomorrow."

"All right, cool, but you good, right?"

"Yeah, I'm fine, just let me shower, and I'll be back." The minute Cash left me alone, I shut the bathroom door, turned the water on and jumped in. The tears started to run down my face as soon as I got in. What was I going to do if I found out this baby wasn't Cash's baby? My life was spiraling out of control, and I had no idea what to do. The air hit my body when the shower curtain opened. When I looked up, Cash was standing there, ass naked, looking at me with sad eyes. He got in and pulled me close to him.

"Baby, why you in here crying?" I had to think of something fast so that it would look like we were on the same page.

"Cash, what will we do with a baby with the way our relationship has been going?"

"Nadia, I will do everything in my power to make sure you and this baby are straight. I also promise to love you the way you need to be loved. Stop crying, we gon' make this work together."

After Cash held me for a little bit longer, I pulled away and looked up at him, and we stared into each other's eyes with so much passion. I then stood up on my tippy toes and kissed Cash on his lips. We engaged in a passionate kiss, and I felt the butterflies in my stomach that I hadn't felt in so long. Cash grabbed my sponge and poured some Dove body wash on it. He then started to wash my body. Once he was done washing me, he washed himself, then rinsed off, and we both got out of the shower. The moment was so tense, and for the first time in our whole relationship, I finally felt like he loved me. This feeling made me want to keep this baby, but then all I kept thinking about was what if this baby wasn't his.

"Cash, I'm scared to be somebody's mother," I said while lying on his chest.

"This is going to be something new for both of us, and we will help each other. Don't worry, Nadia. If you are carrying my seed, baby girl, everything is going to be fine. Do you trust me?" For some reason, the shit he was saying sounded so sincere.

"Yes, I trust you, Cash." I might not have trusted him fully, but him being a good father to our child was a different story. I knew he would be great, but I was still skeptical. I saw how he was with his goddaughter, Luke's daughter, and I also saw how he was with Kyndall each time she was pregnant. So, yeah, I knew he would be great. I just prayed to God that this was his child and no one else's.

I didn't really want to talk about Kyndall, but I was curious if there had been any update on her whereabouts.

"Cash, have y'all heard anything about Kyndall?"

"Nah, I'm supposed to be out looking for her with Luke, but I'm staying in here with you to make sure you good. How are you feeling? Do you wanna go to the hospital tonight?"

"No, I'm OK. I just think I need to get some rest, that's all."

"Are you hungry? Do you want me to go get you something to eat?"

"No, I just want you to stay in this bed and hold me for the rest of the night." Cash smiled at me and kissed my forehead, my nose, then my lips.

"I think I can handle that, but if you need anything else, just let me know, and I'll get it for you."

"I love you, Cashmere."

"I love you, too, baby. Now, be quiet, you making me miss my movie." I looked at him, shook my head and started laughing because he wasn't even watching TV. Tonight felt so good, and I was looking forward to more nights like this. *God, please let this baby be his,* was all I kept telling myself while I drifted off to sleep.

Chapter Seventeen

Shawnee

No one knew where Kyndall was, and we were all going through it. I couldn't believe her ass had just gotten up and left without telling anyone where she was going. This shit was just like Kyndall to run away from her problems, not caring who she hurt in the process. I couldn't wait until I saw her selfish ass. I knew she was going through something, but so was everyone else who loves her.

"Why are you sitting in here like you lost ya best friend?"

"Because I did, Mom-mom Ella. I miss Kyndall with all my heart. How she just gon' leave us like that?"

"Child, that girl needs to find her own way without us. If you keep it up, worrying yourself to death about Kyndall and her life, you gon' lose that good man you got."

"Mom-mom Ella, how can you just sit around all calm like Kyndall is not missing?"

"Because I know she ain't missing. My baby just needed some time to herself, and she'll be straight when she gets back." I guess she was right, but that didn't take away from me being mad at Kyndall's ass. When I see her ass, I'm straight hitting her for having my ass stressed out for the past couple of months.

"Mom-mom, I'm about to go home now."

"Good, you need to, and spend some time with that man. He has been out in the streets day in and day out looking for ya damn cousin because he knows how you feel about her. Not to mention, he had to nurse you back to ya old self when you were starting to go into a depression mode when Kyndall was in that coma."

I wasn't used to Mom-mom telling me to spend time with a dude. She must be feeling Luke. After I kissed her cheek and assured her that I was going to go spend time with Luke, I grabbed my purse and headed out the door. I decided I was going to go home and do a candlelight dinner, but first I needed to stop by the mall and get a new nighty. I also needed some chocolate covered strawberries and enough rose petals to make a big heart in the middle of the bed. I planned to show Luke just how much I appreciated him right now. Mom-mom was right; he sure had been here for me, her, and Cash throughout this whole Kyndall ordeal.

An hour had passed, and I was finally pulling into my driveway. Dinner was going to be chicken stir fry over white rice, so I knew that wasn't going to take long to cook at all. I made sure I had a bottle of Patrón on ice for him, and wine for me. Luke usually came over around eight, and it was now six, which gave me plenty of time to cook dinner, set my room, and shower. Setting the mood, I pulled out my Bluetooth speaker and connected my phone, then threw on my nineties slow jam mix. After I did that, I headed to the kitchen and started dinner.

Two hours later…

There was a knock at my door, and I knew it was Luke. I sprayed Versace yellow diamond perfume on, then headed to answer the front door. I had on a lace nighty with a lace thong, and a silk, hot pink robe. On my feet, I had a pair of hot pink heels that had fur on the top. Giving myself another look in the mirror, my ass was fine as hell. Right before I opened the door, I made sure to leave my robe open. When I pulled the door open, Luke was standing there looking like a whole snack. I wanted to say fuck dinner, and take him straight to the beDreom.

"Damn girl, you look good as fuck."

"Thank you, Luke. Come on in so I can feed you," I said while grabbing his hand and leading him into the dining room. Once he was seated, I walked over to the stove and fixed his plate, then I put it in front of him, poured him a glass of Patrón, and got him a bottled water. After he was set, I fixed my plate, then poured my glass of wine and sat across from him.

"So, what did I do to deserve all of this?"

"Luke, I just wanted to show you how much I appreciate you for being here for me the way you have. I know I've been difficult since this whole thing with Kyndall has been going on, but you still continued to stick by me."

"You're welcome, baby, but it's really no thanks needed. I told you from day one that I had you no matter what. The day you became mine, it also became my duty to be here for you every step of the way." Hearing him say that made my heart skip a beat. This nigga was doing shit to me I wasn't used to.

We sat and ate in silence, then when we were finished, I grabbed his hand and led him to my room where there were rose petals, candles lit, and a bowl of chocolate strawberries sitting in the middle of the bed. He turned around and looked at me, then kissed my lips. I took his shirt off, then unbuttoned his pants, and his monster was already standing at attention. I just couldn't help myself, I had to have him in my mouth. I Dropped to my knees and kissed the head of his dick before I took him into my mouth whole. Luke was enjoying the pleasure I was giving him, and the look on his face was turning me on. I guess I was making it good and sloppy for him. After taking his dick to the back of my throat a couple more times, I decided to show his balls some attention.

"FUCK!" Luke yelled, and right then and there, I felt his body tense up, and he shot all his seeds down my throat. After I gave him head, all I wanted was for him to dick me down. Forget all the foreplay and those damn strawberries. I pushed Luke on the bed, then took his dick back into my mouth to get it hard again. Once it was standing at attention, I planted my feet on the bed, squatted on top of his dick, then slid down slowly.

"Sh-shit, baby!" I yelled. Now that I had adjusted to his size, I was enjoying the ride of my life. Luke and I made love all night in all types of positions. The way he was doing my body, I was sure to be pregnant soon, and I was going to blame Mom-mom Ella for telling me to show him some attention.

Luke

The sun shining through the window woke me up out of my sleep. I looked at my phone and saw that it was eight in the morning. Looking over at Shawnee, she was still sleeping. Last night was everything, and she really did do her thing for a nigga. I didn't think I had ever gotten any treatment like this before. Meia didn't know shit about showing her man attention. Even though most of the foreplay was skipped, I still enjoyed last night.

"Hey, you. Why are you laying there, staring at me like that?"

"Still amazed from last night. I didn't know I had me a freak."

"Shut up, Luke."

"I'm serious, ma. You were doing all kinds of shit last night. You sure you didn't have more than that wine?"

"I'm sure I only had the wine. I just like to please my man. If you weren't my man, you wouldn't have gotten all that special treatment."

"Well, if I can get that all the time, I'ma stay ya man." Shawnee burst out laughing.

"What's ya plans today?"

"Well, I was gon' go back out and look for Kyndall some more."

"Mom-mom Ella said Kyndall ain't missing, so I figured maybe you could chill with Joi and me today since we haven't had a family outing in a minute."

"Yo', I swear I love that about you."

"What do you love about me?"

"Everything, but the way you adapted to my daughter really means so much to me."

"I love her and your mother. They both were so sweet to me from the beginning." I pulled her close to me and kissed her forehead. The minute I pulled her in, my dick bricked up.

"You don' woke the beast up."

"The beast ain't getting none of this kitty this morning. My shit still sore from last night. I ain't fucking with you, Luke. I won't be able to walk out the door today messing with you."

"I'm sorry, baby. You want me to rub it for you?"

"Hell no. It ain't nothing a hot bath can't take care of."

"Baby, you gotta put him back to sleep for me somehow." Shawnee looked at me and shook her head before she went under the covers. The minute I felt her lips peck the head of my dick, I was so ready for her to take me all the way into her mouth. The way she was sucking my dick was even better than last night. Baby girl had my toes curling and everything. She took it out of her mouth, then swallowed real quick in a swift motion. When I felt my head hit her tonsils, it was all over, and I was shooting all my seeds down her throat. After she was finished, she came up from under the covers and kissed my lips, then got up and headed to the bathroom. I just laid there, enjoying the moment. This girl had my head gone already. My phone started ringing, bringing me out of my thoughts.

"What's up, who this?"

"Luke, it's Joi, come quick." I jumped up so quick and threw some clothes on. I didn't know what the fuck was going on, but I didn't like the sound in Meia's voice.

"Luke, what's wrong?" Shawnee asked.

"Meia just called. She said something is wrong with Joi." Shawnee threw on some yoga pants, a t-shirt, and her Air Maxes.

"I'm coming with you." We were both dressed and headed out the door in five minutes. No words were spoken in the car, we just hurried and made it to our destination. I turned a twenty-minute drive to a ten-minute drive; I was scared out my mind. When it comes to my mama and daughter, I was like a little bitch. We were pulling up to Meia's house, and her car was parked out front. I was glad I didn't see any ambulance or cops. Shawnee and I both hopped out of the car and ran to the door. Once we made it in the house, it was quiet as hell, and shit just didn't seem right. I pulled my gun out and headed upstairs.

"I'm going with you," Shawnee said. We were both now on our way upstairs. I had my gun drawn, and Shawnee was right behind me with a metal bat in her hand. When we made it upstairs, all that was heard was moaning. *I know this bitch did not get me with the okey-doke.* I peeked into the room, and Meia was in there, playing with herself. When I tell y'all I was furious, I wanted to shoot this bitch right in her pussy. I walked over to the bed and put the gun to her head. I wanted the stupid bitch to see just how scared I was when she called me, making me think something had happened to my daughter.

"Where the fuck is my daughter, Meia?"

"She's at ya mama's house, Luke. Please don't shoot me."

"Do you know how scared I was when you called me and told me something was wrong with my baby? Bitch, is you stupid? I should blow ya fucking head off right now." Feeling Shawnee grab me around my waist and whisper in my ear kind of soothed me.

"Go get in the car and wait for me. If you kill her, then Joi and I will lose you. Go get in the car, and I'll be out in a minute."

"No, I'll stay here and wait for you." I knew Shawnee was going to beat her ass and guess what, I was letting her do it this time. She grabbed Meia by her hair and pulled her out of bed. She delivered blow after blow to her face. She even kicked her a couple of times. Meia wasn't fighting back, so Shawnee stopped hitting her.

"I'ma tell you this one time and one time only. This man right here, stay away from him. He is no longer any of your concern. Whenever you want Joi, call his mama, and I'll meet you to drop her off. Do we have an understanding?" Meia nodded her head yes, and we left her ass right on the floor bleeding. I couldn't believe this bitch had done this. The crazy part was, I hadn't touched Meia in a long time. When we made it to the car, Shawnee pulled me in for a hug, then kissed my lips.

"I can't believe that bitch did that."

"Relax, baby. I know you're mad, but it's over with now. Let's go to Mama's and see Joi; maybe that'll calm ya nerves." All I kept saying to myself is, *the shit bitches do for the dick.*

Chapter Eighteen

Cash

I had looked all over this city for Kyndall. I had even tried tracing the call when she had called me. It had come from the Hyatt, but they said there wasn't a room booked under her name. It was like I couldn't stop thinking about her. I knew that she was probably OK, I just wanted her to be close to me. Say what you want, but I needed Kyndall around. She was like my happy medium. It had always been that way. She was the reason I was not really in the street like that. She helped me get my life in order. If it weren't for her, my ass would be in somebody's jail.

"Baby, do you want something to eat?" Nadia asked as she walked into the kitchen. I hadn't really eaten anything, but I knew she was going to try and make me eat.

"Yea, can you fix me a sandwich?"

She didn't reply, but I knew she had heard me. I decided to check Kyndall's Facebook to be sure she hadn't posted anything. I just wished I would have said more when she called. I knew I could have gotten her to come to the house.

Nadia brought me the sandwich, and she was fully dressed. It was early as hell. She wasn't a morning person, so that was very odd to me.

"Why you fully dressed this early?"

"Ummm, I'm going to see my grandmom," she lied. One thing about me, I studied the people around me, so I knew when they were switching up. She was for sure doing that.

She only said umm when she couldn't think, and I knew she wasn't expecting me to ask her that.

"OK," was all I said. It was cool because I needed to be out looking for Kyndall. I knew she would get mad, so I let her go and do whatever she was going to do.

I just laid back on the couch and scrolled through Facebook. I was on this girl's page who went to high school with us and spotted a comment from Kyndall. It was made last night, so that let me know she was good. I checked to see if she had read the message I had sent her and they were all unread. That still wouldn't stop me from finding her. I needed to hear her soft laughs and see the way her dimples showed when she smiled. Fuck, I miss her.

After Nadia was gone, I headed to shower. I needed to get myself together so I could go look for Kyndall. I pulled out the Nike sweatsuit that she had bought me a while back and slipped it on. I hadn't worn it because Nadia didn't want me wearing anything that Kyndall bought. She said that Kyndall was trying to buy my love. That was the craziest shit I had ever heard. Kyndall had always bought me stuff.

My phone rang, pulling me from my thoughts. I saw that it was Shawnee, so I answered, hoping she had good news about Kyndall.

"What's up, sis?"

"Nothing, I was checking on you. Luke said you were in your feelings, so I just wanted to see if you wanted to come over and have breakfast with us. Joi requested you."

Joi was my baby, and she knew I would never tell her no. She was such a sweet kid. I hoped that my baby was the same way. I never thought I would be having a baby with Nadia. I knew it was going to hurt Kyndall, and I also knew Luke and Shawnee would be disappointed. Neither of them really cared for Nadia. They said she was a snake, but I didn't see it, though. She did some sneaky shit sometimes, but I think every woman did.

"OK, I'm on the way over." We ended the call, and I headed to Shawnee's house. I had my phone on shuffle and Kehlani came on. That was Kyndall's favorite album, and that was how that shit had gotten on my phone. I changed the song because I knew I was going to get sad thinking about her, and I knew Luke would clown my ass. He knew when something was wrong with me. He was more like my brother than anything. The rest of the ride, I thought about Kyn. It seemed that every time I thought about her, the more I wanted to murk Hakeem's dumb ass.

Once I got to the door, I knocked, then tried the knob. It was unlocked, so I let myself in. As soon as I walked in the door, Joi jumped from behind the couch. I pretended to be scared and crying. She ran to me and rubbed my back and told me that it was going to be OK. Shawnee and Luke were standing in the kitchen, laughing at us. I grabbed her and started to tickle her like I always did. When she started to get down, I put her down, and she ran to the back of the house.

My eyes landed on a picture of Kyndall and me from my birthday last year, and for some reason, tears came to my eyes. I was doing my best to fight the feelings I had for Kyndall, but it was getting harder day by day. I shouldn't have felt this way, but I did. I needed her. I loved her.

"Nigga, I know the hell you not crying." I knew he was going to clown me, but I was at the point where I didn't care. I just wanted Kyndall.

"Fuck you." I went to the bathroom so I could get my shit together. I couldn't believe I was around here, crying and shit. I was a thug-ass nigga, crying wasn't in my blood. Once I felt I was together, I headed back to the front of the house.

Shawnee had shit laid out. She had cooked all kinds of food. "Let me find out you pregnant, Nee," I joked. I needed to get the pressure off of me. They both burst out laughing.

"I know you didn't think I forgot you were just wiping away tears, you crybaby-ass nigga. I can't wait till Kyndall comes back around so I can tell her your ass don' turned into Tyrese, crying and shit. It's cool, I know you miss yo' boo and shit." Luke was really clowning my ass.

"Damn Nee, you gon' let him talk about your brother like that?" I asked like I was hurt. She just laughed and walked off.

Shawnee

I prayed that Kyndall comes back soon because Cash was losing it. I just wished he would admit that he was in love with her. That nigga was missing her something serious. The truth was, I missed her ass, too. She was my diary, and I had so much to tell her.

I was washing my hands so I could get Joi so we could eat when my phone rang. It was an unknown number. I didn't want to answer, but I did.

"Hello?"

"Shawnee." My heart dropped.

"Kyndall, baby, where are you?" I cried. I had been waiting for this call. I knew she would call.

"I'm OK, I just need some time alone, so I can sort things out in my life. How is everyone?" That was just like Kyndall, always worried about someone else when she should be worried about herself.

"Cash is around here going crazy, looking for yo' ass. Luke is good, and so is Joi. Kyndall, can I come and get you, please? I just need to see you. I need to know that you are OK."

"Sis, I'm OK. I just can't face Cash right now. How is Keem?" I was hoping she wouldn't ask about his bitch ass. He was acting like he didn't have a wife who was missing. He hadn't tried to find her. He had moved on with his life like she had never existed.

"I don't know, we haven't heard from him," I stated. I could tell that bothered her, but she didn't say anything.

"Baby, who you talking to?" Luke asked, causing Kyndall to hang up.

"That was Kyn," I stated. Before I had a chance to say anything else, Cash took the phone from my hand like she was still on there. He pulled out his phone and told someone my number. He was quiet for a minute, then he said thanks and ended the call. He handed me my phone and headed for the door. I just turned to go get Joi so we could eat and Luke headed back to the living room.

"Joi, baby, come on so we can say grace and eat." She was sitting on the floor, crying. "What's wrong?" I asked.

"I don't wanna go back home. I wanna stay here with you," she cried. I felt so bad because I couldn't make that decision.

"Luke!" I yelled. He came running into the room with his gun in his hand. When he saw that Joi was crying, his whole demeanor changed.

"Baby, what's wrong?" he asked. Joi was a smart baby, so she knew everything that was going on around her. I just had to tell him the other day he can't say just anything around her.

"I don't wanna go back to my mommy. I wanna stay here with Nee Nee." We planned on letting her spend some time with her mother later today. She had to have heard us talking because we hadn't told her that she was going.

"Why?"

"Mommy mean, and she makes me stay in my room," she cried harder. That shit made me so mad, I wanted to go and beat Meia's ass. Instead, I just walked out the room. I couldn't take her crying. She was really growing on me, and I couldn't take her being hurt.

I fixed our plates, then went and got them. When I walked into the room, Luke was telling her that she could stay with me and that it was OK to love me. That shit made me fall for him harder.

"Let's go eat, baby," I said, interrupting their conversation. Joi jumped up and ran to me. We sat at the table and ate together. That was something I could get used to. I knew these two were my forever, and nothing would change that.

Chapter Nineteen

Kyndall

I felt so much better since I had talked to Shawnee. I knew she was going crazy. I was shocked when she said that Cash had been searching for me. I just knew he was laid up with that hoe Nadia. When they first met, I thought she was cool, but all that changed when she decided she didn't want me and him to be close.

I knew Luke was going to tell him I had called, so I hung up. Hopefully, she didn't tell Luke that it was me calling. Since I had talked to Shawnee and Mom-mom Ella, I headed to take a shower. I planned on going down to the casino to try my luck. I had been in my room since the day I got here.

Just as I was getting out the shower, I heard a knock at the door. I hadn't asked for any room service, so I had no idea who it could be. I put on my robe and opened the door. My heart dropped. There was no way he had found me.

"Cash, wh—" He didn't give me time to finish my sentence before kissing me. The kiss was so passionate. We had never kissed before, and I was stuck. It was like I couldn't pull away, like my body needed this. It was refreshing, like a cold bottle of water on a hot summer day.

"How did you find me?" I asked as soon as I was able to pull away.

"Kyn, don't you ever leave me like that again," was all he said. He looked me in my eyes and my body melted by the second.

I was about to reply when he pulled me closer to him and hugged me. My center was dripping. It was on from that point. He stuck his hand under the robe and rubbed his finger across my throbbing clit. That shit felt amazing. He untied my robe, and I let it fall to the floor. He took my right breast into his mouth, and my knees buckled. His kiss was so soft. He undressed me while he gave my right breast the same attention he gave my left one.

Once he was undressed, he picked me up and laid me on the bed. I knew that what we were doing was wrong, but it was too late to turn back.

"Kyndall, I love you," he said, kissing me once again.

"I love you, too," I managed to get out in between kisses.

He climbed on top of me, and I could feel him at my opening. Our eyes locked, and as he made his way inside of me, I didn't think my body had ever felt like this before. Keem and I fucked day in and day out, but he never made love to me.

"Oh my God, Cash. I'm cumming," I moaned. He was stroking me nice and slow, but each time, he was hitting my spot.

"Shit, Kyn, baby, your shit so tight. Fuck."

Once I got used to his size, I started moving my hips so I could match his strokes. I guess I was getting the best of him because he flipped me over without even pulling out. That had to be some new shit. His ass didn't miss a beat.

He made sure I had the perfect arch and went to work. I knew when he was done, I wasn't going to be able to walk.

"Just like that, Kyn, baby. Throw that ass back," he demanded. I did as I was told until I felt his body go stiff. I knew what that meant. He released inside of me, and we both collapsed on the bed.

He got up and went to the bathroom, and I just stared at the ceiling. I knew I should have stopped him, but it was done now, and I needed to know where his head was. I got up to see if he was OK because he had been in there a while.

"Cash," I called out before opening the door.

"What's up?" he replied, coming closer to me. He looked like a Greek god. His dreads were hanging in front of his face, and his body was dripping wet. I wanted to jump right back on his dick.

"What did we just do?" I asked. I prayed that he had an answer for me because I was lost.

"We just made love," he replied, turning to me. I could see the love in his eyes. I had never seen that in Keem's eyes when he looked at me.

"Where do we go from here?"

"I don't know."

Hakeem

I was home, sitting on the couch, watching SportsCenter, and sipping on a beer. It was really starting to get to me that no one knew where my wife was. As I was starting to get in my feelings, I heard the front door open. I looked up and saw it was Kyndall. I ran over to her and pulled her in for a hug.

"Baby, where have you been?"

"Oh, so you really cared where I was, or are you just asking because you see me?"

"Come on, Kyndall, baby, don't do me like that. I've been going through it since you've been gone."

"After I go shower and slip on something comfortable, I think we need to talk." No matter what y'all think about me, I still love my wife with all my heart. I just made bad decisions and choices that I wish I hadn't made. Now, I was willing to try and make our marriage work, I just needed to figure out what to do with Chrissy's whining ass. After about an hour, Kyndall came downstairs. I swear my wife was so beautiful, and it wasn't until this very moment that I realized I'd been missing her like crazy. I think that was why I had been snapping on Chrissy lately.

"Keem, I'm really disappointed in how our marriage has been going. We both have been all broken up over the loss of our child, but baby, we need to do better. I don't know who it is outside of this marriage that has your attention, but you need to end it right here, right now. I love you with every breath in me, but I will no longer sit around and let you shit on me, Keem. I'm in a different head space right now, and I'm not just settling. So, if you think you can't handle being with just me, then you might as well step. I ain't in the business of keeping a man who don't wanna be kept. When we said our vows, we said for better or worse, and that's the only reason I'm here today."

"Kyndall, I'm sorry, baby, and I promise you, I'ma do better. I love you, too, and I want our marriage back the way it was. We've been going through so much, we haven't even grieved our baby girl."

"Keem, I grieved, got depressed and grieved some more, so, baby, don't tell me I didn't grieve because I did. I just did that shit alone when my husband should have been here by my side every step of the way. I don't know who she is, but if you don't cut shit off with her, we are done, and I'm taking you for all you got, and I mean that shit, Keem. Depression is a motherfucker, but that shit sure has made me wake the fuck up." Yeah, my wife was different, and she sounded like she wasn't about to play with my ass. Just as I was about to say something, my phone started to ring. She just gave me a side-eye, then got up to head in the kitchen.

"Keem, go ahead and answer it and tell the bitch your wife is back home, so stop calling your phone. Then when you hang up, call Sprint and change your number, please." Once I picked up the phone, I knew it was Chrissy's crazy ass because I'd been trying to avoid her ass, but she wouldn't leave me the hell alone.

"Don't call my phone no more."

"Keem, please don't play with me. I'm telling you, you really don't want these problems."

"Listen, my wife is home, so don't call my phone no more." I knew Chrissy's ass was batshit crazy, but hell, with the way Kyndall was looking, her ass was just as bad. I'd figure some shit out with Chrissy real soon, but for the time being, I hoped she didn't cause any problems. Kyndall was still in the kitchen, so I went to see what she was doing. She was in front of the sink, starting to prepare something to eat. I knew I was trying my luck, but I missed touching my wife. I walked up behind her, wrapped my arms around her waist, and nuzzled my nose on the side of her neck. To my surprise, she didn't stop me or move my hands. All she did was rest the back of her head on my chest.

"I know I haven't been the best husband, and I promise you I'ma do better."

"Show me don't just tell me. Keem, you've hurt me to the core, but the love I have for you is why I stay. You were supposed to be and stay my everything. We took vows to always stay together for better or worse, and you can't seem to stick it out when I'm at my worst. Our best friend has my back more than you, and he has his relationship to worry about instead of being in ours all the time. Another man should not be worrying about my well being more than the man who said he would always love and cherish me."

The shit Kyndall was spitting today had me feeling like a real fuck boy. She was right. I was always supposed to love and cherish her, no matter the situation. I had let her not being able to give me a kid fuck up our whole marriage. Right now, she was giving me a chance to make things right, but I had done the ultimate betrayal and gone out and made a baby on her. When she finds out, she is never going to forgive me. How could I be so fucking stupid? I had a prize package at home, and just because she couldn't conceive, I'd done all types of shit. Then I went out and cheated with two women who were not even on Kyndall's level. This shit was all types of crazy, and I hoped and prayed that she didn't find out about Chrissy before I figured out what to do.

Chapter Twenty

Chrissy

"Arghhhhh!" Feeling overwhelmed and frustrated, I threw my phone across the room. Keem had been ignoring me for a couple of days, which meant his little Kyndall must have been back home. I had been praying day in and day out that her ass was somewhere dead so I could have him all to myself, but like always, shit never worked in my favor. I'd been calling him like crazy, and he wasn't answering, then the minute he did answer, he told me not to call him because his wife was back home. I didn't know how he expected me to just allow him to do what he wanted to do when he wanted to. I was the one who could carry his baby, so why wouldn't he love me? I was so in my feelings, the tears were falling down my face.

"Chrissy, what the fuck you in here crying for?" Dre barked.

"Why won't he love me the way I want him to?"

"Come on, Chrissy, you already knew a baby wasn't going to keep that man. If he treated his wife the way he did, what made you think he was going to treat you any different? Men ain't shit, take it from me. I'm a man who ain't shit sometimes, but I love my wife. If she was to call me out on half the shit I do right now and threaten to leave me, my bitch ass would cut all the side chicks off."

"Well, why bother to cheat if you love her like you say?"

"Because some men ain't shit, Chrissy. A lot of us ain't get that player out of us yet. We get that one chick we want to tie down, and we know we not ready to settle down yet, but we still do it so we won't lose the one we want. It sounds fucked up, but that's life. You deserve so much more, baby sis. You need to stop crying over that nigga and know your worth, mama," Dre assured me. I knew Dre was right, but shit, I wasn't trying to hear that. Keem might not want to be with me, but he and his precious little wife would be taking care of this baby. Shit, it wasn't like they were taking care of any kids of their own. As a matter of fact, she might not ever give him one, anyway.

"Dre, I wish I could just give up that easy, but I just can't. There is a baby involved now."

"There's a baby involved, but let's not forget, women take care of babies alone every day. All you did was make the single mother rate a little higher, that's all, sis."

"FUCK YOU! What are you here for anyway?"

"Don't get mad at me because I done kept it real with ya stupid ass. You better hope that nigga don't get killed once they find out he been stealing they money."

"He didn't steal their money, you did."

"I did, but why? Because you asked me to set him up. How do you think he gon' feel after he finds out you set him up? Hell, I know how you gon' feel, single as fuck," Dre said while cracking up.

"Dre, get the hell out of my house."

"Don't worry, I was leaving anyway. I'm about to take my wife shopping since I have a couple of extra dollars." Dre left out, and I sat on the couch, crying my eyes out.

When Keem found out what I had done, he was going to kill me. I had only done it because he was playing with my emotions like he was doing once again. This whole situation was getting on my damn nerves, but if I couldn't be happy, no one would. Keem had woken up a raging beast in me, and if he thought his wife was back to stay, he had another thing coming. See, when everything is out in the open, little precious Kyndall was going to be so hurt. If I couldn't have him, then she wouldn't, either, and if Keem didn't want me, we could both be single and co-parent. I was going to make sure no one got a fucking happily ever after. Dre's ass was on the shit list, too. Let me find out who he is messing with so I can tell his little Suzy homemaker as well. Shit, we were all going to be some miserable-ass folks when I was finished.

After crying for a little bit longer, I decided to take care of my hygiene, and head out to do a little shopping, courtesy of Keem. His stupid ass had been so caught in his thoughts, he hadn't even realized I had stolen his card out of his wallet.

＊＊＊＊＊＊＊＊＊＊＊

I was walking around Cherry Hill Mall, trying to figure out what else I wanted. I didn't feel like I had put a big enough dent in Keem's card just yet. As soon as I walked past the food court, I saw Dre and Cash's girl. I only knew it was her because I remembered seeing her and Cash come by the office sometimes. These two were dumb and bold as hell. Like, who the hell would be creeping in the mall? I knew they had something going on because I could see Dre rubbing her leg under the table. This shit just added to my plan a little more. After spying on them a little while longer, I left to get a new phone since I had broken mine by throwing it at the wall earlier today.

Walking into the Sprint store, seeing Kyndall and Keem angered me to the fullest. The look on his face was priceless, and all I could do was smile. Keem tried to hurry and walk by, but I had a trick for his ass.

"Well, hello, Mr. and Mrs. Richardson."

"Hello, Chrissy, how are you?" Kyndall asked with a big smile on her face.

"I'm great, just trying to get a phone. I heard that iPhone X is dope."

"Yeah, it is, but it's a little pricey," Kyndall assured me.

"It is, but bae gave me the card for the day, so I have been spending like crazy." Kyndall laughed while Keem gave me the death stare. Yeah, he was probably mad at me saying bae, but wait until that nigga saw his bank statement.

"All right, well, go do you, love. It was nice seeing you today." Kyndall was dumb as hell for not noticing how quiet Keem was. That shit was crazy as hell. I would have questioned that. After they left, I went ahead and got my phone, a case, extra charger, and some wireless earbuds.

Cash

I hadn't been able to get Kyndall out of my head since we'd made love. Every five minutes, thoughts of that day kept running through my head. The crazy part about it was she wouldn't answer my calls or respond to my text messages.

"Baby, what's wrong? You seem so distant today," Nadia asked while straddling me.

"I'm good, ma. How are you feeling today? When are we going to the doctor?"

"They gave me an appointment for Friday morning. Are you gonna be able to make it?"

"Of course, Nadia. I wouldn't miss that for the world." She smiled at me, then started placing soft kisses on my neck. It seemed like after I had made love to Kyndall, she was all I'd been wanting. I knew it had been a couple of days since I had fucked Nadia, so if I pushed her away, there was going to be a problem.

"CASH, don't you hear me calling you?"

"My fault, ma, what's good?"

"Cash, I'm sitting here, trying to get some dick and you in another world. There's something going on with you, but you ain't telling me. Not to mention, ya dick ain't even getting hard, and I was grinding on you the whole time. Who the fuck is she, Cash?"

"What are you talking about, ma? What you mean, who is she?"

"Cash, don't fucking play with me, nigga. Your body wasn't even reacting to me. It's like you didn't give a damn about me just now."

"Nadia, I don't wanna argue with you, mama. Every time I turn around, we arguing, and I'm sick of it."

"Cash, you know what, fuck you. We wouldn't always be arguing if you weren't doing me wrong. I'm out, and don't call me to come the fuck back. When I'm gone, you want me, but when I'm here in ya face, you don't wanna be bothered. I'm so sick of trying to figure out how to please Cash when he doesn't wanna do the same for me. Maybe we just not good for each other." Nadia wanted me to say some hateful shit to her, but I wasn't. I let her fuss and storm off like she always did, but this time, I was going to have somebody on her ass. I needed to know her every move since she was pregnant with my seed.

Twenty minutes later, she came back downstairs fully dressed with her favorite Gucci duffle bag, headed for the door.

"Be safe out there, and don't be doing no stupid shit with my baby in ya stomach, Nadia. I'll see you Friday for the appointment. Text me the address. Don't forget I got this city on lock, so if I wanna find you, I will." I winked at her crazy ass and laid on my couch. Shit, maybe I needed a couple of days away from her. I couldn't seem to get my head straight after I had fucked Kyndall.

"Yo, bro, what's going on with her hoe ass? She almost knocked me down, running out of the door," Luke asked, walking in.

"Man, she tripping. What are you doing here?"

"You were supposed to come by the warehouse today, and you never made it. What's going on with you, bro? You haven't seemed like yaself for the past couple of days." I sat up and put my head in my hands, and Luke knew something was up.

"I fucked up big time, now my head all fucked up." Luke gave me the side-eye and shook his head.

"What happened? Talk to me, bro."

"For starters, Nadia's ass is pregnant, and all we do is argue, man. How we supposed to bring a kid up in this crazy shit we got going on? I mean, I'm happy about it, but we ain't ready. Like, financially, you already know we good, but our relationship ain't healthy."

"My opinion on that situation is to get a blood test because I don't trust the hoe, and if it's yours, take the baby." Luke had never liked or trusted Nadia. I swear my boy didn't like many people, and that shit was crazy.

"That ain't all, bro. The day I went to get Kyndall from AC, we fucked." Luke looked at me, shook his head and started laughing.

"Damn Cash, I know y'all got feelings for each other, but you just made this shit hella complicated. Baby girl is still married, and she just tried to kill herself. Not to mention, you have a girl who is now pregnant. Y'all got too much shit going on. You know sex complicates shit big time."

"I know, man, but at the time, I was missing her so much, and I had to have her. Now she's not answering my phone calls or text messages."

"That's because she's confused, man, and she probably feels like y'all ruined y'all friendship. So let me guess, that's why Nadia left."

"She was mad because she was trying to fuck and I was in a daze, not paying her any mind. Then she said she was grinding on me, and my dick wasn't hard. The minute my mans didn't react to her, she asked me what chick I was fucking."

"Damn, Kyndall put that shit on you like that? The shit got ya mind gone. I don't like Nadia, but she had every reason to be mad."

"I know, man. I fucked up big time. Then she said when she's gone, I want her home, but when she's home, I act like I don't wanna be bothered. All her years of complaining about Kyndall was true; I'm really in love with that girl. The shit I'm feeling is some shit I ain't ever felt before, and it seems like the shit got worse after we slept together."

"Nigga, you in love, that's what that shit is, but I don't know how this shit gon' work out. She's still married to Dick Head, and Nadia's hoe ass is pregnant."

"Not just that, Luke. The chick Keem fucking with is pregnant. Remember we were fighting about it at the hospital? When she finds that out, it's gon' break her heart, and the fact that I knew and didn't tell her is gonna make matters worse." All this shit was crazy, and a nigga didn't have a clue how to handle it. One thing I did know was that I had strong feelings for Kyndall, and I didn't regret what we had done.

Chapter twenty-one

Nadia

Cash had me fucked up if he thought I didn't know what the fuck was going on with him. Ever since they had found little miss Kyndall, he had been acting funny. It was cool, though. Since she had my nigga's mind occupied, I was going to do the same to her nigga. They both had me fucked up. As soon as I got in the car, I called Keem, and to my surprise, that nigga had changed his number, and that let me know that he was at home with that bitch Kyndall. So, I decided to go to my house for a change. See, Cash thought I had let it go because I was at his house so much, but he was mistaken. I still had my own shit. There was no way I was going to be left with nothing. What he didn't know was that I was putting up money every time he gave me money. On top of that, Dre was giving me money, and so were a few other niggas I was fucking with. My bank account was sitting nice.

It felt good to be at my own shit. I went straight to the shower. The hot water was giving me life. It felt nothing like Cash's shower, though. Once I was done in the shower, I texted Dre. I needed to nut bad.

Me: *Come and get this pussy.*

I knew he was going to come running; that nigga was worse than Keem. He didn't care where we fucked. Shit, the other day, we fucked in the bathroom at the mall, and that was some of the best I'd had from him.

Dre: *Where are you?*

Me: *My house.*

Dre: On my way.

I went to the kitchen, so I could fix something to eat. I had just eaten when I was at Cash's house, but I was hungry again. This baby was going to have my ass fat. It seemed all I did was eat.

I laid out on the couch and decided I would call my sister since I hadn't talked to her in a few months. I didn't call her often because she was all church-y and shit. She had married a preacher, and they had moved to Ohio.

"To what do I owe this pleasure?" she answered.

"I just wanted to check on you and see what you were doing," I stated.

"Oh, you didn't want to check on your daughter?" I knew she was going to say that shit. She was always throwing my daughter in my face, and that was one of the reasons I didn't call her ass. She had taken my baby, then she got mad that I didn't come see her or call. Hell, if she wouldn't have taken her, she would be with me.

I thought about telling her that I was pregnant again, but I knew she would go off. My sister had raised me after my mom got on drugs real bad. It was just her and me for as long as I could remember. She was all I knew until I got in the streets. My daughter, Nya, is five. She had been living with my sister since the day I had her. My sister was always mad at me, but she should have let me get an abortion, then she wouldn't be stuck with my baby.

"How is she?" I asked. I loved her, but I just wasn't ready to be anyone's mother. The only reason I was having this baby was because I knew I would be financially set for life. Cash would make sure of that. I just had to make sure he thought this baby was his without a doubt. Honestly, I thought it was Keem's baby, but I was not sure.

"Good. She started school this year, and she's doing really good. You should come see her," Monica recommended.

"I will see what I can do, but I was just checking on y'all. Someone is at my door so I will call you later," I told her as I ended the call before she had a chance to say anything.

I knew it was Dre at the door, so I adjusted my robe, so it hung off my shoulder. I wanted him to get straight to it. I wanted my nut so I could send him back to his wife.

"Damn baby, I see you ready for me," he said, adjusting his dick in his pants. That was one of the things I hated to see men do. I stood to the side so he could come in. As soon as the door closed, he was all over me. I was doing my best to be into it, but I couldn't, I wanted Cash. It was like my body was fiending for him.

I hadn't even realized that Dre had slipped his dick into me, my mind was somewhere else. I moaned because I knew that would make him nut fast. I just wanted this nigga out my house. This was going to be the last time I fucked with him. I needed to get my shit in order before Cash found out what I'd been up to.

Once he nutted, I walked him to the door without saying a word. I knew he was going to be in his feelings, but I didn't care, I wasn't his bitch. I locked my door and headed to take another shower. All I wanted to do was go to sleep.

Luke

I didn't know what Cash had thought when he had sex with Kyndall. He knew that was a disaster waiting to happen. What he didn't know was that he had made things way harder for himself. At this point, he didn't have any choice but to be with her because their friendship would never be the same.

We sat and talked for a little over an hour. I looked at the clock, so I knew I needed to go and collect my money so I could get home to my woman and daughter.

"Aye, nigga, I'm about to roll. I gotta go do pickups."

"I'ma roll with you." Yeah, this nigga was bugging. I couldn't remember the last time he had stepped foot into a trap house. I just nodded and headed for the door. As soon as I made it to the car, he was coming out the house. Once he was in the car, I headed to the hood. It took me no time to get there since there wasn't much traffic. I noticed that the only car that was there belonged to this nigga named Jon-Jon.

"What that look mean?" Cash asked as he made sure he had his strap.

"Dre not here. He knows it's time for the count. That nigga has been fucking up lately. I don't know what's up with him," I stated as we headed for the door. When I walked in, I got pissed. It looked like they'd had a party or some shit. I knew Cash trusted me, but I didn't want him to think I wasn't running shit the way I should have been. Although I oversaw shit, this was still his empire, and I didn't want him to regret letting me take over.

"Yo, why the fuck my shit look like this?" Cash yelled, causing Jon-Jon to jump. I just stood back because I knew some shit was about to go down. I think people sometimes forget Cash is a savage.

"Umm, Dre just left a while ago. Look, I don't know what's going on. I was chillin like I always do."

"So, let me ask you this. Who in this motherfucker working because you not on my payroll?" I questioned. I took a seat on the arm of the couch so I could hear his response loud and clear.

"Dre been paying me. He said you was cool with it. Shit, I was just trying to make a little extra money. I wasn't trying to step on no toes." I knew it wasn't his fault that Dre wasn't here, but Cash wasn't going to see it that way.

"Go get my money," Cash demanded. Jon-Jon jumped up and ran to the back of the house. I looked at Cash, and I knew shit was about to get worse. I could see it in his eyes.

Jon-Jon came with the bag of money and Cash cleared the table so he could count it. The house was quiet as hell, and all you could hear was the sound of the money rubbing against his hand. When I counted the last dollar, he took a deep breath. I knew what that meant.

"Call a meeting tonight. I want everyone at the warehouse in an hour," was all he said before walking out the door. I bagged the money up before telling Jon-Jon he needed to be there since he was the one who was here when we got here. I just hoped he listened because I would hate to have to kill him. He was a good dude.

I was sitting back, watching Cash pace the floor. I kind of regretted letting him come because I knew he was already going through some shit. All he was going to do was take his anger out on these folks.

"Why do people want to play with my money? I have been trying to sit back and let shit take its course, but that shit is over. I know Keem is the one who is stealing from me, but Dre's ass is looking a little suspect, too. I want to wait until I have both of them together so I can see what's really good," he stated calmly. I didn't say anything because no matter what I thought, this was his shit.

A short while after, they all started filing in. "Who all works in that house?" he asked.

"Dre, Smooth and Marc." He nodded. I knew then one them was about to feel that nigga's wrath. They were all having side conversations. They had no idea what kind of danger they were in.

"So, I want to know why my money is short?" he asked, causing the room to get quiet. Everyone was looking at me, but there was nothing I could do to help. I had been saving niggas for a while now, and all of that was over.

"So, no one has an answer for me? Dre, what you think?" Dre looked like he was about to shit his pants. The crazy thing was, he knew Dre had something to do with it, he just wanted to see if the nigga was going to man up.

"Shit, it was good when I left."

"From now on, the count will be done every day by Luke or me. No one is to leave until one of us is there. That goes for you, too, Dre." They all just nodded. "I'm going to make some changes in the next few weeks. I see that since

I'm not around, y'all think this shit is a game. Well, I'm here to tell y'all it's not."

I looked up, and this cat named Spanky was smiling. I just shook my head. I just hoped he told his family he loved him because he was going to make it home.

"I wanna laugh, too," Cash yelled, causing the smile that was on his face to fade. He was new, so he didn't know the type of nigga Cash was. Every time he saw Cash, he was dressed in a suit. "Tell me what's funny."

"Nothing. I was reading a text from this li'l bitch," his dumb ass said. The whole room looked at his ass like he had three heads.

Before he had a chance to brace himself, Cash's fist smashed into his face. Blood went everywhere. I wanted to stop Cash, but I knew he needed to release some of his anger. By the time Cash stopped hitting him, there was blood all over the room. That nigga's face was smashed in. You would have thought a truck had run him over.

"Clean this shit up, and nobody better leave this motherfucker until my money is counted." He walked to his office, and I was right behind him.

"Why the fuck won't she answer!" he yelled, knocking everything off his desk. I just stood back because I would have to have to shoot his ass; there was no way I was going to try and fight with him.

He grabbed a bottle of Remy and started drinking it straight. I had never seen him like this. All I could do was call Shawnee. I knew she would know what to do to calm him down.

Chapter Twenty- two

Shawnee

I was sleeping good as hell until my phone rang. I was just about to get mad until I realized it was Luke's ringtone.

"What up, baby?" I answered.

"Baby, I need you to come to the warehouse. This nigga losing it, and I don't know what to do. See if you can get Kyndall to come, and don't tell Keem where y'all going." I jumped out of bed and put some clothes on.

"I'm on the way," was all I said before ending the call. As soon as I was in the car, I called Kyndall. I knew she was probably in bed.

"Hey, boo." I was happy as hell that she had answered.

"I'm finna come get you. Luke said Cash is spazzing out, and you know you the only one who can calm his crazy ass down."

"I don't think that'll be a good idea. I'm trying to work on my marriage, and Cash is a distraction," she stated.

"Are you fucking serious, Kyndall? Cash is always there for you, and he was there when that sorry-ass husband of yours wasn't, and you just put him on the back burner like that?"

"I get what you saying, but I just can't right now. You know him just like I know him, Shawnee," she mumbled. I knew she was probably talking low because Keem was there. I didn't give a fuck, she was going to see about Cash whether she wanted to or not.

"Bitch, I'm on the way. All he needs to do is see your face, and he will calm down. Be ready when I get there, and don't tell him where you going," was all I said before I ended the call.

I didn't know what the fuck was going on with them, but they needed to get that shit together. Hell, she had made me mad talking about working on a marriage with that bitch-ass nigga who didn't give a fuck about her. He just didn't want Cash to have her.

I called her phone when I was pulling up on her street so she could come outside. When I pulled into her driveway, she was standing there, looking mad, but I didn't care.

Before she could get in the car good, I was pulling off. I didn't need his ass coming out the door, being fake and shit.

"So, what the hell is wrong?" she asked with an attitude. I rolled my eyes because she was pissing me off.

"What's up with you, Kyn? I don't like the way you been acting," I added. She had been through a lot, but damn.

"I just know me and him don't need to be around each other. We are both trying to work on our relationships." I could tell there was more to that story, but I was going to let it ride today. The rest of the ride was quiet as hell. I guess she was in her feelings.

When we pulled up to the warehouse, there were no cars there but Luke's. I parked, and we headed for the door. We headed to the back where the offices were, and just as we were walking in the door, a Remy bottle flew past our faces. Cash's office was a mess; there was shit everywhere. Kyndall just stood there and watched him punch holes in the wall. Luke was standing outside of the office, playing fucking Candy Crush on his phone like this shit was normal.

I watched as Kyndall slowly made her way into his office. When she made it over to him, she touched his shoulder, and he instantly stopped punching the wall. He didn't even see her walk up, but he knew it was her. That shit was crazy as hell.

"That's some creepy-ass shit," Luke said from behind me.

"Yea, it is."

His hand was dripping with blood, so she ripped a piece of the t-shirt she was wearing and grabbed his hand, then wrapped it. The minute he fully realized Kyndall was actually standing in front of him, he pulled her in for a hug. This nigga's face was weird as hell, but I guess they were both starting to realize how much they loved one another.

Kyndall

After looking into Cash's eyes, all the feelings from the day we had made love came right back. The whole time I was home, it was out of sight and out of mind. Now, I couldn't get him out of my mind. As soon as I calmed him down and wrapped his hands up, I was good and ready to leave. Cash wouldn't let me go. He felt the need to sit and tell me how he really felt, finally, and now my mind was so clouded. I knew my feelings were the same, I just wasn't ready to admit it. I was trying to get my marriage in line.

"Baby, what's wrong? You've been in another world since Shawnee Dropped you off. Where did y'all go?"

"I told you we had to check on Mom-mom Ella. She's not feeling well." I didn't know how many times I had told him that since I'd been home, but it was like he didn't believe me. It was like he thought my story was going to change.

"I don't know if I believe that, but all I know is if you want me to change and be a better person, that means you need to do the same. Don't let me find out you lying to me, Kyndall." No this nigga didn't just try to come for me. As many times as his ass had lied to my face, he better get his life because he was about to make me click out on his ass.

"Listen here, Keem, don't you ever try to act like I've been lying after all the shit you've done to me. Not to mention, I'm still tryna make this marriage work when I should have left ya no-good ass. I was gone for almost two weeks, and not one time did you try and find me, and don't lie and say you did because I know better. You could have called the phone company. The phones are in your name. You could have easily found out what they changed my number to, but you didn't because you were too busy worried about yo' side bitch." After I read his ass, I got up and headed to our bedroom. All this shit that was going on was taking a toll on me. I was trying to keep from going into depression mode again, but I was on edge.

"Kyndall, baby, I'm sorry. I didn't mean to piss you off. We are in a better place right now, and we don't need to be at each other's throats."

"Have I ever given you a reason not to trust me?"

"No, Kyndall, you haven't, but there's just something about the way you and Cash act towards each other lately." This was the first time Keem had ever said anything about Cash and me.

"All the years we've been together, you have never had a problem with Cash and me. What's really going on, Keem? Why the sudden feelings?"

"I don't know, Kyndall, I guess I see the way he looks at you, and the way he's always jumping to your rescue."

"This is crazy, Keem. He's not only been here for me, but he has also been here for you as well. All the times we've lost babies, he has been here for the both of us. So, since when does it mean anything when a friend has your back?"

"You're right, Kyndall, it doesn't mean anything, and he has been there for both of us."

"What happened to y'all two while I was in a coma? Y'all seem so distant. I just wish things were the way they were when we were in college."

"We got into an argument because he felt like I hadn't been there for you enough." I knew it was more to the story, but I also knew he wouldn't tell me the truth.

"So, Keem, tell me, why weren't you there like you should have been? It felt like a slap in the face not waking up to my husband holding my hand, waiting for me. It really made me feel unloved. I was up for a whole week, and you were nowhere to be found. Why is that?" Sitting here reliving all of this made me feel some type of way, and the tears started to fall. *How could he not be there for me? We had made a vow in front of God.*

"Come on, baby, please don't cry. It hurt me to see you like that."

"That's not a fucking excuse, Keem. No matter how much it would have hurt me, I would have been there with you. You know what, Keem, just leave me alone. I don't want to talk about it. I need to go out and get some air." He put his hand up as if he was surrendering, and let me walk by him.

"Kyndall, I'm sorry, baby. Go ahead and get some air. I'll be right here when you get back." I grabbed my car keys and purse, then headed out the door. The minute I made it to my car, I pulled out my phone and sent Cash a text.

Me: Meet me at Cooper River Park.

Cash: All right, I'm on my way.

I knew this wasn't a good move, but I also knew I could always talk to Cash without him judging me. Right now, I needed someone who was going to just listen, and that was Cash. Shawnee or Mom-mom Ella would both go off on me for even considering making my marriage work.

Pulling into the parking lot at the park, I noticed Cash was already sitting there. I jumped out of my car and headed for him. Once I tapped on the window, he opened the door, and I climbed in.

"What's good, beautiful?"

"Hey, you. How you feeling after last night?"

"I'm good, baby, and thanks for coming to calm me down. I don't know what had gotten into me. What brings you out the house?"

"I asked Keem why y'all weren't talking, and he said because he wasn't there for me like he should have been. What's really going on Cash?"

"He told you already. I was having a hard time dealing with him not being by your side, and we got into a fight in the hospital." I had a feeling they were both hiding something from me, but I was going to leave it alone because what happens in the dark always comes to light. I didn't say anything else, I just left it alone.

"So, where's Nadia? I haven't heard you mention her."

"We are going through it right now, but she'll be back."

"Do you really want her back?"

"Come on, Kyn, you already know who I want, so stop playing, ma."

"I know, Cash, but you know I'm trying to make my marriage work." I saw the sadness in his eyes as soon as I said that. I regretted even letting it come out of my mouth.

"If that's what it is, Kyn, why call me when y'all going through something? This shit is starting to get to me, ma. If

I can't have you, I would rather not be around you. This shit is kind of killing me inside, especially since I know he's not gon' do right by you."

"See, Cash, this is why we shouldn't have slept together. Now our friendship is not going to be the same. I don't know if I can take losing you as a friend, Cash."

"Losing me as a friend is not happening, so you might as well figure out how we gon' work this shit out," Cash said while grabbing my face and pulling me in for a kiss. The way the kiss made me feel, I ended up straddling him, and he leaned his seat all the way back. The next thing I knew, I was shirtless and riding his dick right in the car. Thank God the windows were tinted. Here I was, once again, putting myself in a compromising situation. I was trying to make my marriage work, but how could I do that when I was in love with my best friend?

Chapter Twenty-three

Hakeem

Kyndall thought I was stupid, but I was far from that. See, my wife and Cash always talked to each other, no matter what, but lately, she'd been trying to avoid him. I knew she had said it had to do with his relationship with Nadia, but I wasn't buying that shit. I was on my way out the door to follow Kyndall but got a surprise.

"So, you changed your number on me like we don't have a baby on the way, Hakeem?" Hearing her scream my name all loud had me pissed. I had to hurry and push her stupid ass in the house before my neighbors heard her.

"Chrissy, what are you doing here? What if my wife was here?"

"I knew she wasn't here because I've been following her stupid ass. You need to teach her dumb ass how to check her surroundings." This crazy bitch was out of control, following my wife and shit. That was the shit you see on TV, and it kind of creeped me out.

"Come on, Chrissy. Why are you tripping, ma?"

"You the one tripping, nigga. You think I'ma just let you live happily ever after while I'm out here, sad and missing you. Not to mention, we have a baby coming in about six and a half months.Yeah, you heard right, nigga; I'm almost four months. I didn't even know I was that far along. I went to the doctor and told them I was feeling movement already, so they did an emergency ultrasound. My last period wasn't matching up with how far along they thought I was. They told me I must have been getting my cycle at the beginning of my pregnancy, which threw me off." I was sitting in shock, thinking about all of this. I had to have a seat and take it all in. While I was sitting, I took a good look at Chrissy, and I could see her pudge. This meant she was pregnant when Kyndall was. My wife was really going to kick my ass out. Even though shit was all fucked up, the joy of knowing I was about to be a father came over me.

"Come here, ma." I called Chrissy over to me and started rubbing and kissing her stomach. While I was kissing her stomach, she grabbed my face with her hands, then leaned down and kissed my lips. I couldn't help myself, I pulled her down on my lap. My dick was already at attention, and she had a dress on. It was a wrap when I realized she didn't have any panties on. I slid her sexy ass on my dick. She had to get adjusted to my size, like always, but once she was, baby girl rode the shit out of my dick.

"FUCK! Chrissy, ride that dick, ma."

"Keem, baby, I've missed you so much, baby. You feel so good inside of me," Chrissy moaned in my ear. I swear I needed this nut. Kyndall and I hadn't had sex since we'd been trying to make things work. The minute Kyndall came to mind, my dick got soft. *What the fuck am I doing, fucking Chrissy in my crib, on the couch, knowing Kyndall could be walking in at any time?*

"Dammit Chrissy, you have to go, ma." I removed her from me, and the scowl on her face told me she wanted to kill me.

"What the fuck is wrong with you, Keem? You ain't never did any shit like this to me."

"Chrissy, you have to go. My wife might walk in at any minute."

"You know what, Keem, fuck you and ya wife. You swear she worried about you and me. I told you I was following her ass, and that's why I came here. I knew she was already occupied by someone else, so I figured I would come and occupy you. Trust me, she's having some fun of her own with that sexy-ass nigga, and the way the car was moving, they were probably doing the same thing we were doing. Only, she probably got her nut." What she said had me ready to kill her ass. Here I was, once again, with my hand wrapped around her throat.

"Chrissy, stop lying. You didn't see my wife with no damn man." She was struggling to talk, so I decided to let her go so I could hear what she had to say. Before she spoke, she had to gasp for air from me choking her.

"I followed her to Cooper River Park. That's where she met Cash. If you don't believe me, go check it out yourself."

"Come on, ya ass gotta go."

"Why, because you about to go find ya little wife?"

"Chrissy, just take ya ass home, and I'll be there as soon as I handle something." Her face lit right up when I told her I would see her later. I knew I had to lie to her in order for her to leave me alone. I walked her to the car and kissed her lips. I swear her ass was as dumb as a doorknob. I had choked her ass up, and she still wanted me to come fuck her. Shaking my head, I made my way to my car so I could see what my pretty little wife was up to.

Chrissy

Keem had to be out of his mind if he thought I was going home. I wanted to see this shit play out. He pulled out so fast, he didn't even wait to see if I was going to go the other way, which was good for me. I waited until he pulled off, then I followed him. He was driving like a bat out of hell. I was glad that I knew where I was going because otherwise, I would have lost him. Just as I was getting caught up to Keem, my phone rang. When I saw that it was my brother, I hit ignore because I knew what he wanted. As soon as I was going to power my phone off, it rang again, and I made a mistake and answered.

"Bitch, I know you been seeing me calling you. Why the fuck did you tell my wife that bullshit?" his voice roared through my car.

"I bet you'll think twice the next time you try me. I know you value her just like I value Keem. Now, either you can stop framing him, or I can send all of these pictures I got of you and yo' side bitch. It's your choice, so I advise you to choose wisely," I told him. See, he had always looked at me like I was weak. My whole life, he had run over me, but that was all over now. This was going to be the last time he did this shit to me. I couldn't understand for the life of me, why he couldn't just get his own money. My brother had a degree, but he was too lazy to grind like others do.

"How could you do that shit to me? Renee is my wife, not some bitch I was fucking. You assisted in breaking her heart, Chrissy. What have you turned into? You are not my sister. She would never do that." I could hear the hurt in his voice. I felt bad because I knew I had fucked up with the one person who had always had my best interest in mind.

"I love you, Dre, but I want my baby to grow up better than we did. He may not be with me, but trust me, we will get far more money out of him this way. I know for sure this is his baby so he will have no choice," I explained. He was quiet, so I knew he was thinking about what I had said.

"You need to fucking make this shit right with Renee. I can't lose her, Chrissy." He sounded like he was going to cry, and that alone killed me. I was getting ready to reply, but I realized he had hung up on me. I was pulling into the park, so that was fine. I would just call him when I got done busting up this family reunion.

Cash

"Cash, where do we go from here? We can't keep sneaking around," Kyndall told me as we sat on top of my car. It was getting dark, so the sky was beautiful.

"I don't know, you could just move in with me," I joked. I knew that wasn't going to happen, but I was taking my shot. I knew she cared about Keem.

"I'm not finna play with you, Cash. Just give me some time, and I will figure it out," she said as she kissed me. This shit was life. I had to have her, and I was going to do whatever it took to make her mine.

"Have you told Shawnee about us?" I asked. I knew Luke knew, but I was also sure he hadn't told Shawnee. I knew she was going to be mad we hadn't told her. She had been rooting for us for years.

"Hell no, I will never hear the end of that. Her ass be blowing shit out of proportion. She'll be ready to tell the whole world." She wasn't lying. Shawnee's ass had a big mouth when it comes to everybody's business but hers. I knew she meant well, though. She was all about Kyndall being happy, and that was all that mattered to me. I loved the relationship they had; it was like me and Luke's friendship.

"I love you, Kyndall."

"I love you, too, Cashmere." She kissed me, and my dick got hard instantly. That is until I heard the last voice I needed to hear.

"Damn, so Naida wasn't lying; y'all really are fucking," Keem said as he walked up to my car. I knew he was going to try and act tough. I just laughed. We all knew his soft ass wasn't about that life. He knew I could beat his ass with my eyes closed.

"Keem, I can explain." I didn't know why she was trying to explain to his ass. He was the one who had been fucking around on her with other bitches and getting them pregnant. Not to mention, I still owed his ass for stealing from me. He better tread lightly.

"You don't need to explain shit to him. Truth be told, he needs to be explaining some shit to you." I knew I shouldn't have said that, but she needed to know that she was married to a bitch-ass nigga.

"What does that mean?" she asked, looking from me to Keem.

"That I'm giving him something you couldn't," Chrissy said, walking up to where we were. I looked over to Kyndall, and I saw that look on her face again.

"Stop, just fucking stop. Cash, did you know this?" She had tears rolling down her face. I didn't want to answer her because I knew it would hurt her. I Dropped my head. I couldn't look at her. It made me regret not telling her when she first woke up, but I just wasn't that type of nigga. I wanted him to be the one who told her.

"Yep, he knew," Chrissy blurted. I wanted to beat her ass.

"I didn't ask you anything. Why did you even come here? What type of woman wants to see another woman hurt like this? And Keem, I knew you had fucked someone, but I would have never thought it was her. Chrissy, you looked in my face and spoke to me the other day and knew that you were fucking my husband."

"Bitch, please. You shouldn't be mad anyway, you were just fucking another nigga. Shit, his best friend at that. And, trust me, I wasn't the only one fucking him. Isn't that right, baby daddy? Tell her who else you fucking," Chrissy said while looking at me. This bitch was crazy. Who does shit like this? This was one of the reasons I didn't cheat. Side bitches didn't know their damn place.

"Chrissy, I told you to go home. Why did you come here?" Keem asked. I was wondering the same thing. What she didn't know was that she was just making shit harder on herself. If he was avoiding her, he really wasn't going to fuck with her after this shit. I wanted to knock her ass out, but my hand was throbbing. I knew that my next stop was going to be the hospital. I hadn't gone last night because Kyndall had wrapped it up well, but it was bleeding now. I guess when I was trying to grip her waist, I had hit it. I was so into her, I didn't think about my hand.

"Who else are you fucking, Keem?" Kyndall asked. He was quiet as hell. I knew he wasn't fucking Shawnee because she damn near hated that nigga, so who the hell mattered that much that she was making it her business to let Kyndall know?

"You can tell them, or I will. Better yet, let's not waste any more time. Let's just put it all on the table. Keem, tell yo' best friend how you been fucking his girl for the past few months."

As soon as the words left her mouth, I pulled my gun out. I blacked out. I couldn't believe what the fuck I had just heard. There was no way she was telling the truth. I knew me and Kyndall were wrong, but damn, that nigga had been fucking my bitch and stealing from me. Without looking, I let off three shots. When I turned around, I could have died at the sight in front of me. I knew from that moment; my life would never be the same.

To be continued...

www.ingramcontent.com/pod-product-compliance
Lightning Source LLC
Chambersburg PA
CBHW061449150726
47987CB00001B/382